" 'CRIMES OF THE HEART' IS PURE FRESH AIR. Beth Henley is a warm, humane, funny and shrewd writer with her own voice."
—Jack Kroll, *Newsweek*

"This is a tale of three sisters. One is a spinster, one is a sexpot, and one is a screwball. The tangled web of relationships they weave possesses sprightly humor, zany logic, folksy warmth and a tincture of poignancy . . . antic in spirit . . . beguiling."—*Time*

"OVERFLOWS WITH INFECTIOUS HIGH SPIRITS . . . A PERFECT FUNHOUSE!"
—Frank Rich, *The New York Times*

"THE MOST ADORABLE TRAGI-COMEDY . . . IT HAS HEART, WIT AND ZANY PASSION."—Clive Barnes, *The New York Post*

"OFFBEAT AND COMPLETELY CAPTIVATING . . . *Crimes of the Heart* is crammed to the top rim of the pickle barrel with accurately observed human foibles, as well as the kind of ear for the way Southerners sound and talk and act that could only be learned from eavesdropping."
—Rex Reed, *The New York Daily News*

The above is a small sampling of the extraordinary praise given the triumphant, Pulitzer Prize-winning play, Crimes of the Heart. *Now its love, warmth and exhilarating humor are expanded beyond the limits of the stage and screen in a sensitive and spirited novel that will make you laugh and cry along with those irresistible Magrath sisters.*

CRIMES OF THE HEART

A Novel by

CLAUDIA REILLY

Based on the Screenplay by

BETH HENLEY

A SIGNET BOOK

NEW AMERICAN LIBRARY

The play CRIMES OF THE HEART by Beth Henley was produced on the Broadway stage by Warner Theatre Productions, Inc./ Claire Nichtern, Mary Lea Johnson, Martin Richards and Francine Lefrak.

CRIMES OF THE HEART was given its New York premiere by the Manhattan Theatre Club in 1980.

Originally produced by Actors Theatre of Louisville, Inc., February, 1979.

PUBLISHER'S NOTE

SIGNET TRADEMARK REG. U.S. PAT. OFF. AND FOREIGN COUNTRIES
REGISTERED TRADEMARK—MARCA REGISTRADA
HECHO EN CHICAGO, U.S.A.

SIGNET, SIGNET CLASSIC, MENTOR, ONYX, PLUME, MERIDIAN and NAL BOOKS are published by New American Library, 1633 Broadway, New York, New York 10019

First Printing, December, 1986

1 2 3 4 5 6 7 8 9

PRINTED IN THE UNITED STATES OF AMERICA

One

Immediately after their local picture show closed down, the residents of Hazlehurst, Mississippi, returned to the simple pleasures of life—going to church, drinking too much, and gossiping. Especially gossiping. Up and down the dusty streets that led away from the town square, men and women idled away evenings on the porches of their clean, white-painted houses, glasses of bourbon in their hands, tales of neighbors' lives in their mouths: *"You know that pretty Johnston girl who works over at Piggly Wiggly?" "The one with the mustache?" "That's the one. Well, now I was talking with Hettie Pheiller, and* she *says how* she *heard that the girl's got herelf a full sprout of chest hair, too." "No!"* "Yes!" *"Well, isn't that just the most disgusting thing."*

Almost any subject that could be rendered halfway scandalous was mined for conversation, though talk about physical deformities and behavioral eccentricities were the mainstay of Hazlehurst gossip. Everybody knew Lenny Magrath couldn't have babies on account of her deformed ovary, that Doc Porter walked the way he did because he'd survived a hurricane ordeal, that Chick Boyle's children brought used birthday presents to parties because their mother was cheap, not poor, and that Mrs. Thompson giggled in that peculiar high-pitched tone at funeral ceremonies because she was insane. Other subjects of gossip interest included traffic accidents (*"You see that squirrel over by the highway? Why twenty people must've run the poor thing over. Like wall-to-wall carpeting, it was."*) and health problems (*"They say Emma Knight's brain tumor's gettin' so big even her husband's taken to screamin' when she removes her hat."*) Yet while such gruesome matters turned up in most daily conversations, one topic clearly was Gossip King: the bizarre, blood curdling murder committed by Mary Magrath just moments prior to her own equally horrifying suicide.

The crimes had taken place sixteen years back in nearby Vicksburg, but that didn't prevent Hazlehurst's citizens from acting as though they had happened yesterday and in their own town. Even the smallest children knew the story by heart: Mary, who had grown up in Hazlehurst, had started to get more and more peculiar after her good-for-nothing husband walked out on her. She began ignoring her three little girls—Lenny, Meg, and Babe—and had spent her days sitting on her porch steps slinging cigarette ashes down at the ants that crawled over her feet. Finally, after giving up eating and sleeping and even changing her clothes, she had walked slowly down the steps to her cellar, where she calmly proceeded to do things so perverse and mysterious that even the most hardened of crime reporters expressed revulsion when they arrived on the scene.

Every newspaper in the country carried an account of the freakish event, and when Mary's daughters moved to Hazlehurst to live with their grandfather, TV reporters descended on the tiny town in hopes of getting a juicy interview with the children. That proved impossible, for their grandfather kept the girls hidden from the glare of the cameras. The reporters then turned to the townspeople to try to dig up the awful truth. Why had Mary done what she'd done? Had she been insane? Evil? Possessed by some unearthly demon?

The citizens of Hazlehurst didn't know any more than the reporters. But while the reporters soon gave up on the mystery of the killing and returned to their newspaper offices and television stations, the townspeople had nowhere to go, nothing much to do except go over the story time and time again, trying to make some sense of it.

In an effort to keep the Magrath saga alive and Hazlehurst on the map, many townspeople had also turned their talk to Mary's daughters. Every move the Magrath girls made was noted with the keen interest usually reserved for celebrities. *"Wouldn't be surprised at all,"* folks would say, *"if one of those girls doesn't grow up to inherit her mama's bad blood. There's something strange about those Magrath children."*

But years went by, and the girls became women, and not one of them showed an inclination for murder and mayhem. Babe, the youngest and prettiest of the three, even managed to enter the esteemed inner circle of Hazlehurst society after marrying the town's wealthiest man.

Meg, the wildest of the girls and thus the one most people thought would follow in her mother's footsteps, moved to Hollywood in search of fame and fortune as a singer, while Lenny, the mousiest of the girls, became a spinster dedicated to the care of her grandfather.

And then came the day when twenty-four-year-old Babe was spotted getting out of a police car with handcuffs attached to her dainty wrists. Her big blue eyes sparkled; her strawberry-blond curls blew in a late May breeze; her rosy mouth curved up in a happy, glad-to-be-alive-in-springtime kind of smile. All in all, she seemed utterly oblivious to the fact that her expensive, lacy pink dress was covered with great quantities of her husband Zackery's blood.

Lenny Magrath, Babe's eldest sister, and Lucille Botrelle, Babe's sister-in-law, were standing in the master bedroom of the Botrelle family's ancestral home, a cream-colored, five-story mansion built in the Greek revival style. It sounded much grander than it appeared, for it actually resembled a tastelessly overdecorated wedding cake.

Lucille, a fifty-two-year-old woman who might have become a prison matron if she hadn't been born exceptionally rich, had spent years working on her reputation as Hazlehurst's most forbidding personality, and was reaping the fruits of her labor. She had news about her brother Zackery's health which Lenny desperately needed to know, but rather than give forth the doctor's report, she chose to stand stonily beside an enormous canopy bed at the room's center and stare at Lenny with an expression most people only use for dogs who have just wet on priceless rugs.

Lenny trembled before Lucille's glaring eyes, but then Lenny had a tendency to tremble before anyone's eyes. She was a desperately nervous young woman who was still as slumped and shy as she had been back in high school when she was an ugly duckling who had spent long hours at dances trying to pretend it didn't matter that boys never asked her to take a twirl in their arms. That she had ceased to be homely didn't occur to Lenny, especially now that her dreaded thirtieth birthday had arrived. When she looked in a mirror, she didn't see her wide hazel eyes, her glowing brown hair, or her fine, strong body. Instead she saw a withering crone destined to remain a spinster until death mercifully came to collect her.

Lucille made a peculiar snorting noise as Lenny opened up a small white suitcase and laid it across the canopy bed. Lenny had come to the Botrelle mansion to collect clothes for Babe to wear home from prison after her bail was set later in the day. It was not an easy task to stand before a woman like Lucille and pack up Babe's things, and Lenny's heart began to pound so hard and fast that she half expected the buttons on her plain, overwashed sweater to shoot across the room.

Don't let her see how scared you are, Lenny told herself as she lifted a one-eyed teddy bear and set it into the suitcase. Try to handle this the way Meg would. For Meg, the middle Magrath sister, never let anyone intimidate her.

And while Meg's ability to stand her ground had often created a lot of friction within the family, Lenny knew that Meg would be better at handling someone like Lucille than she herself could ever hope to be. If Meg were present, Lenny knew she would march straight up to Lucille and say, "Okay, you old witch. So tell me what the doctor said. Is Zackery dead or what?"

But Lenny couldn't do that. Even thinking about doing such a thing terrified her and made her shoulders slouch even lower. It was impossible to handle this crisis like Meg. For Meg, always first-asked at school dances, lived in the World of Glamorous Girls as far as Lenny was concerned. Meg was a curvy starlet out in Hollywood, not a noodle-shaped brickyard worker in Hazlehurst like Lenny. Meg was one of those women whose confidence in herself was as high as her list of marriage proposals was long. She didn't understand how impossible it was to stand up to people like Lucille when you knew for a fact that even the fattest and ugliest of men didn't want you for a wife on account of your ovary problem. So what difference did it make how Meg would deal with Lucille? Lenny was just going to have to keep packing the suitcase, and in time Lucille would get tired of making her feel like a dustbunny and would tell her what the doctor had to say.

Lenny hurried about the room, packing up the case and reviewing all the horrible events that had transpired over the last twenty-four hours. First of all, yesterday morning she had learned that a blood vessel had popped in her grandfather's brain. That made something like five or six over the last few weeks. So she had called Babe to tell her the horrible news, only to reach a policeman who had even worse news for Lenny: Babe was being held at the local jail for the attempted murder of her husband. At first Lenny thought it had to be a joke, but when she got down to the jail, there was Babe sitting behind bars. Lenny had hurriedly asked what was going on, but Babe was keeping her mouth shut and wouldn't even speak to the lawyer their uncle had hired. All Lenny really knew for sure was that Zackery was lying in the hospital with his stomach full of bullet holes and that Babe was being formally charged with the crime.

Lenny sighed, walked over to an antique bureau, and opened a drawer full of soft, pink clothes.

Lucille decided to speak. "The damage to the spinal column has not yet been determined." Each word fell from her mouth like ice cubes from a tray.

The statement felt like a kick in the head to Lenny. Weren't spinal column injuries the very worst injuries of all? Wasn't it almost better to be dead than to live out your days as one of those quadri-whatevers that had to be rotated like chickens on a rotisserie in order to keep from getting huge, gaping bedsores? Lenny hurled some of the pink clothes into the suitcase and scurried to pack up Babe's saxophone so that Lucille might not see the terror in her eyes.

But Lucille did see it, and she had to fight

back an impulse to smile. Sucking in her already prunelike cheeks, she said, "But his breathing's been stabilized and the liver's been saved."

Lenny nodded weakly as she lifted the saxophone into a battered black case. "Well," she whispered, attempting to inject a note of optimism, "that's good news."

The pupils in Lucille's eyes turned enormous with anger and her nostrils flared like a challenged stallion's. "None of this is good news, Lenny Magrath. It's all a grueling nightmare. And mark my words, those responsible will pay dearly."

Lenny opened her mouth to respond to Lucille's threat but couldn't think of anything intelligent to say. In a moment Lucille was gone, banging out of the room in a huff, and Lenny was alone with the half-packed suitcase, the old saxophone, and the uneasy conviction that today was not only going to be the worst birthday of her life, but also the worst *day* of her life. It had started off even worse than the day Mama had done the ghastly thing that Lenny tried never to think about, because it not only made her sad, it made her nauseous. Yet at least on that terrible day, all three of the sisters had been together, which had somehow made everything bearable for Lenny. Today, each of them was alone—Lenny in the frightening Botrelle mansion, Meg somewhere absolutely unreachable in Hollywood, and Babe . . . sweet, freckle-faced, cute-as-a-button Babe. Well, just thinking about where Babe was made Lenny want to shriek in horror.

She bit down on her lower lip to keep from

crying out, something she was still doing fifteen minutes later when she loaded the suitcase and saxophone into her ancient Ford. Lucille, to Lenny's relief, had chosen to keep herself hidden after she had left the bedroom. But as Lenny steered her car down the steep hill that separated the Botrelles from the rest of Hazlehurst's families, she had the eerie feeling that Lucille was watching her from a window.

Certainly, everyone else in town *was* peeking out windows at Lenny. Driving slowly, nervously to a grocery store on the square, Lenny watched her neighbors watching her, pointing her out to one another. And inside the grocery, as she stood in line holding a package of panty hose for her cousin Chick and a box of birthday candles for herself, she could hear whispers all around her: *"Is that the killer?" "No, that's the one with the ovary problem."*

Things will be better when I get home, Lenny thought, and indeed when she finally pulled her car up the gravel driveway of her grandfather's house, she felt her body start to relax. "Home," she said to herself, as though the word held magical powers of healing.

The Magrath house had a tumbling-down look to it, but what it lacked in upkeep it more than made up for in charm. It was a Victorian creation, with two swirling towers, a gingerbread gazebo latticed with ivy, a wide and sunny side porch, and yellow and purple stained-glass windows that gave every room the look of springtime at dawn. Ever since Lenny had moved to Hazlehurst, she had loved this house, especially its lush backyard with perennials blooming like crazy and its craggly oak tree with a rope swing dangling from one of its twisted limbs. There was also a beautiful, flowering magnolia tree, beneath which Lenny, Meg, and Babe had spent so many years of their childhood, hiding from neighbors' prying questions, playing Barbie dolls and beauty parlor, spinning out tales of who they would be and what they would do when they grew up. Then, in their teens, they had taken their talk inside to the kitchen, where they had sat at a rickety, white-painted table filling their mouths with popcorn and Cokes. They had talked about everything—or at least everything but Mama.

Opening the kitchen screen door, Lenny eyed the table, and a great sense of loss washed over her as she looked at the chair where Babe had always sat. Lenny, as the oldest of the sisters, had always thought it her duty to keep conversation away from the subject of Mama. But maybe if she and Meg had spoken things through with Babe, all of what was happening now might have been prevented. Maybe there was some connection between this new tragedy and Mama. . . .

Suddenly Lenny began to feel nauseous. Obviously thinking about Mama wasn't going to help. But what would?

Lenny set down the suitcase, saxophone, and grocery bag. She was just about to start biting her lower lip again when a hopeful notion swept over her. My birthday candles, she thought, and her face lit up for the first time all morning as she realized that she had a birthday wish due her. Not that any of her previous wishes—

for a husband, for a normal ovary, for happiness in general—had ever come true, but you never knew. There was always a first time.

After giving a quick glance at the screen door to make sure she was alone, Lenny ran to a cookie jar on the kitchen counter and grabbed the biggest cookie she could find. Then she darted to the stove for a box of matches. Soon she was ripping open the box of candles and trying to make one of them stand upright on her cookie.

Unfortunately, the candle wouldn't stay put. It kept careening off the cookie, toppling this way and that. So Lenny tried to jam the candle in to hold it firm, but that only made the cookie shatter.

Lenny looked up in frustration. Here she was, incapable of even making a birthday wish. Surely life couldn't get any worse.

But, of course, life can always get worse, and Lenny's was about to do precisely that, for as she sat at the table destroying her pathetic birthday cookie, her cousin Chick was preparing to visit. And Chick had a way of making even the bleakest of days seem a little bleaker.

If anyone had asked Charlene "Chick" Boyle if she hated her Magrath cousins, she would have vehemently shaken her small, yellow-haired head and insisted that she pitied the poor things. She pitied Lenny for being a frump, pitied Meg for being white trash, and pitied Babe for being what Chick had once thought was mildly retarded but now suspected was murderously insane. "*Hatred* is not a word in my vocabulary,"

Chick was fond of saying to her husband Buck, a person she also pitied—in his case for being so deranged as to want to have sexual intercourse even though he and Chick already had as many children as they wanted.

No, I don't hate anyone or anything, Chick thought as she stood in her yard, supposedly checking to see if any of her flowers were ready for picking but actually waiting for her cousin Lenny's car to pull up the next-door driveway. I am a good Christian fully prepared to do my duty by my relatives, even if those relatives happen to be disgusting people who do things that make my skin crawl.

When Lenny's car finally did make an appearance, Chick's skinny, poultrylike arms began to flail and she started screeching orders to her maid, Annie May Jenkins: "Annie May! I'm on my way! Now you be sure to defrost that chicken for supper. There's a can of Vienna sausages in the cupboard for your lunch. Fix peanut butter and jelly for the kids."

Annie May, a sullen-faced black girl who liked Chick about as much as she liked diarrhea, sat in the kitchen of the Boyle family's fussy, knick-knack-filled house and ignored every word Chick—who by now was racing to the Magraths' house—shouted at her. As for Chick's children, redheaded Buck Jr. and equally redheaded Peekay, they too ignored their mother's voice as they stood behind Annie May shooting toy arrows at their pets. The pets yelped and howled and ran from the room while Chick carried on with her instructions: "Now, whatever you do, Annie May, don't let the children get ahold of any matches or combustible explosives. I don't want any repeats of last week's near-fatal disaster. Is that clear?"

Chick stood for a moment in the Magraths' overgrown yard waiting for a response from Annie May. She licked her bright red lips and brushed a hand through her curly, beauty-parlor-styled hairdo. Annie May, as usual, didn't even have the decency to call back a "Yes, Mrs. Boyle." Well, Chick thought, what can I expect from someone whose ancestors no doubt spent their lives swinging through trees?

Chick hurried up the back steps to Lenny's door. "Lenny! Ooooh, Lenny!"

Lenny jumped at the sound of her cousin's screechy voice and hurriedly stuffed the cookie and candle into her sweater pocket. It would be just like Chick to see them and make fun of her for celebrating her birthday in such a lonely, pathetic manner.

"Hi," Lenny said weakly as Chick ripped open the door and burst into the kitchen.

Chick didn't see any reason to mince words. "It's just too awful," she began. "It's just *way* too awful. How I'm gonna continue holding my head up high in this community, I do not know." And then, letting her head drop low to illustrate her point, she caught sight of a rip in her stockings and added, "Did you remember to pick up those panty hose for me?"

"They're in the sack."

Chick snatched the panty hose from the paper bag and began pulling her own stockings down. "Daddy has called me twice already. He says we gotta get ourselves to town t'help take care of this thing with Babe before they change their simple minds."

Lenny had to turn away from the sight of her cousin's legs, which looked to her as white and pasty as dough. Staring at the cookie bin, she listened for a moment to Chick's pantings as she struggled to get her stockings down to her knees, then quietly said, "I was hoping Meg would call."

"Meg!" Chick shrieked breathlessly, the stockings now at her ankles.

"I sent her a telegram about Babe and—"

"A *telegram*!" Chick squeeled, kicking the stockings across the kitchen floor. "Couldn't you just phone her up?"

"Well, no," Lenny said, " 'cause her phone's out of order."

Chick opened the new pair of panty hose with a snort. "Out of order?"

"Disconnected," Lenny allowed. "I don't know what."

Tossing the cellophane and cardboard from the panty hose somewhere in the vicinity of her old stockings, Chick gave Lenny a condescending smile. "Well, that sounds like Meg."

Lenny opened her mouth. She wanted to speak up on Meg's behalf, wanted to say that Meg wasn't the sort of person who ignored phone bills and got her phone disconnected, but since Meg was that sort of person, what could she say? So she closed her mouth and looked at the cardboard and dirty stockings on her floor. She knew her cousin intended to leave them there for her to clean up.

Chick was inching the new panty hose onto

her toes. "So just what all did you say in this 'telegram' to Meg?"

"I, well, I just told her to come on home."

Chick froze with studied horror. "To come on home! Listen, Lenora, Babe's gonna be incurring some mighty negative publicity around this town, and Meg's appearance isn't going to help out a bit."

Again, Lenny felt the impulse to rush to her sister's defense, but again she didn't see how. If she were to ask Chick why Meg's return to Hazlehurst would stir up trouble, Chick would just give her a hundred reasons, many of them good ones.

Lenny glanced at her cousin. Chick was doing a peculiar kind of knock-kneed snake dance as she struggled to raise the panty hose over her thighs.

Chick caught Lenny's eye and grimaced. "My, these are snug. Are you sure you bought my right size?"

"Size extra petite."

Chick shook her head with puzzlement. "Well, they're skimping on the nylon material," she said, beginning to sweat as the panty hose climbed slowly over her derriere.

At last, weak and weary, Chick was able to get the panty hose hoisted to the point where her waist had once been. She let out a slow breath and returned to the subject at hand. "Anyway, Meg is known all over Copiah County as cheap Christmas trash. Why the whole town knows about her dealings in that sordid affair with Doc Porter, leaving him a cripple."

This time Lenny did defend Meg. "A cripple? He's got a limp. Just kind of. Barely a limp."

"Well his mother was going to keep me out of the Ladies' Social League because of it."

Lenny, who knew this story by heart, hoped she wasn't going to have to hear it again. "Oh please, Chick," she said. "But you're in the Ladies' League now."

Chick reached into her bright red purse for a hairbrush, assenting to the fact that she had managed to squeeze into the club despite being first cousin to Meg Magrath. "But frankly," she said as she teased her hair to an alarming height, "if Mrs. Porter hadn't developed that tumor in her bladder, I wouldn't be in the club today, much less a committee head."

For a moment, the kitchen was silent as Chick's eyes clouded over with the memory of how close she had come to being a social outcast. She shivered as she realized that life was indeed lived on the razor's edge. But soon she was able to turn her mind from such deep philosophical concerns by forcing her thoughts back to the here and now. "Anyway," she told Lenny, "you stay right here and wait for Meg to call so's you can convince her not to come back home."

Lenny said nothing.

Chick took this as agreement and smiled. "So how's my hair?"

Lenny eyed the travesty on her cousin's head. "Fine."

"Not pooching out in the back?"

"No."

"All right then," Chick said, cleaning her hairbrush with her fingers. "I'm on my way."

Lenny watched as Chick casually dropped

the hair from her brush onto the floor, but said nothing. If she was going to clean up Chick's stockings, she might as well clean up her hairballs, too. And anyhow, there was no time to even think of saying something to Chick. Already, as Chick was putting her brush back into her purse, she was squealing about something else.

"Oh! Oh! Oh! I almost forgot," Chick shrieked, yanking a gaily wrapped box from her purse. "Here's a present for you. Happy birthday to Lenny from the Buck Boyles."

Lenny took the box from Chick's magnanimous hands and said, "Why thank you, Chick. It's so nice to have you remember my birthday every year like you do."

Chick managed a lousy imitation of a modest smile. "Oh, well, now, that's just the way I am, I suppose. That's just the way *I* was brought up to be," she said, still recalling a time seven years back when Lenny had forgotten *her* birthday. "Well, why don't you go on and open it?"

"All right," Lenny said, and started to remove a piece of tape from the wrapping paper.

But Chick couldn't contain herself. "It's a box of candy. Assorted cremes."

"Candy," Lenny said, not sure whether to bother opening the present now or not. "That's always a nice gift."

Too nice for you, Chick thought. Out loud she said, "Oh, speaking of which, remember that little polka-dot dress you got Peekay for her fifth birthday last month?"

Lenny remembered the dress vividly. She had spent all her month's lunch money on the little outfit. It was just the sort of thing she would have wanted to buy for her own daughter. If she had a daughter. If she had a husband. If her ovary weren't deformed. "The red and white one?"

"Yes," Chick said agreeably. "Well, the first time I put it in the washing machine—I mean the very first time—it fell all to pieces. Those little polka dots just dropped right off in the water."

Lenny felt as though an ice pick had been thrust into her chest. "Oh no! Well . . . I'll get her something else then. A little toy?"

"Oh no, no, no, no, *no*!" Chick insisted. "We wouldn't hear of it. I just wanted to let you know so you wouldn't go and waste any more of your hard-earned money on that make of dress. Those inexpensive brands just don't hold up."

Just then both women heard the rumble of tires coming up the gravel driveway and turned toward the kitchen window to see Doc Porter getting out of his pickup truck.

Doc was an attractive man, worn from hard work and hard living so that he looked somewhat older than his thirty years, but not so worn that women didn't still think he was the most handsome fellow walking the streets of Hazlehurst. He looked as he always did, brown hair slightly mussed, faded flannel shirt rolled to his tanned elbows, and cotton khaki pants a little wrinkled. He walked with a slight limp, but his manner of walking—maybe just a tad slow—only added to his appeal.

To Lenny's way of thinking, Doc was the

most perfect man who had ever lived—tall, strong, steady. He was always so confident and willing to take the time to make other people feel just as confident. Back when Doc and Meg had dated, Lenny liked to be the one to open the door and chat with him while Meg fussed upstairs with her clothes and makeup. Back then, Doc had had a way of looking at Lenny that took away her shyness and made her sit up straight. She had always felt alive in his company, so happy and secure. But then Meg would come down the steps and Doc would forget Lenny existed.

Lenny watched Doc take a sack of pecans from his truck as Chick went to the door. "Why look," Chick called out in a voice she reserved for men she found handsome. "It's Doc Porter!"

Chick scurried out to the yard and Lenny followed her.

"Well how in the world are you doing?" Chick asked Doc, her eyes taking in his bad leg.

Doc just smiled. He knew better than to try to get a word in edgewise with Chick on the premises.

Chick leaned toward him and confidentially explained, "I can't stay. I've got some people waiting on me." And then, as though it were a secret, "It's all this business with Babe."

Doc nodded and grinned at Lenny as Chick thrust back her shoulders like Napoleon about to do battle. "Well," she sighed, "farewell and good-bye." And then she was racing giddily to her own house, her arms flapping in the breeze, her new panty hose already starting to run in the back.

" 'Bye," Lenny called.

Chick ignored her.

Doc glanced around the yard and then smiled at Lenny. "Hello."

Lenny smiled back bashfully. She felt peculiar standing alone with Doc. Even though she kept her horse, Billy Boy, over on Doc's land, she conducted her business dealings about the horse with Doc's wife. It had been hard to talk to Doc ever since he and Meg had broken up.

"I guess you heard about the thing with Babe," Lenny said.

"Yeah." And then, a little nervously, "Lenny?"

"What?"

"Uh . . ."

Lenny looked up at Doc's eyes, but he turned away from her. She waited a moment, and yet he still didn't say anything. Finally, she broke the silence. "Yes?"

Doc started to say something, stopped, and then thrust the pecans toward her. "Here. Some pecans for you."

Lenny took the pecans and peeked into the bag. "Why thank you, Doc. I love pecans."

Doc nodded. "My wife and Scotty picked them up around the yard," he said, staring down at his feet.

Why he seems almost as nervous talking to me as I am talking to him, Lenny thought. This surprised her because Doc just wasn't the sort of person to be anxious with people. "Well," she said, trying to calm him with conversation the way he had once calmed her, "I can use them to bake a pie."

Doc said nothing.

"A pecan pie," Lenny added helplessly.

"Yeah," Doc said at last. And then, glancing at her with sad eyes, "Lenny, I've got some bad news for you."

Lenny swallowed hard. "What?"

"Well, last night Billy Boy died."

Lenny couldn't quite take in the words. Feeling as though she was lost in some bad dream, she whispered, "He died?"

"Uh-huh," Doc said, as gently as he could. "He was struck by lightning yesterday."

Lenny's whisper turned to a croak. "Struck by lightning?"

Doc nodded sheepishly.

"In that storm yesterday?"

"That's what we think," Doc said.

Lenny's eyes began to brown out on her. She stumbled toward a trellis swing in the yard and sat down. Doc walked after her.

"Gosh," Lenny said, hoping that sitting down might prevent her from fainting. "I've had Billy Boy for so long. You know? Ever since I was ten years old."

Doc sat down beside her and pushed the swing with his feet. "Yeah," he said, at a loss. "He was a mighty old horse."

Stung to the core by Doc's unconscious reference to her own age, Lenny could only repeat his words. "Mighty . . . old."

For a time she and Doc creaked back and forth on the swing. So Babe was in prison, Old Grandaddy was in the hospital with his blood vessels popping, and Billy Boy—Lenny's only real, true-blue friend—was dead. He's dead and I'm thirty, Lenny thought, looking at her hands and wondering how long it would be before they were covered with age spots.

At last, Lenny made an attempt to rally herself. "Hey," she said cheerfully, "today's my birthday. Did you know that?"

"No," Doc said. "Happy birthday."

"Thanks," Lenny said, trying not to think about Billy Boy or old age or Mama or Babe or Old Grandaddy or . . .

Lenny began sobbing uncontrollably.

Doc turned to her, a little embarrassed. "Oh come on now, Lenny. Hey, now. You know I can't stand it when you Magrath women start to cry. You know it just gets to me."

Lenny stood up from the swing and dragged herself across the yard. She wanted to stop crying, wanted to pull herself together and be strong, but her tears were getting worse. "Oh-ho! Sure! You mean when Meg cries! Meg's the one you could never stand to see cry. Not me! I could fill up a pig's trough." And with that said Lenny turned to the mimosa tree and wrapped herself around its smooth, slim trunk.

Doc eyed her for a moment. He knew she was having a rough time of things. He also knew that she had always been jealous of his relationship with Meg. "Now Lenny," he said, as kindly as he could, "stop it. Come on. Jesus."

Lenny let go of the tree and nodded. She wiped at her eyes, and sniffed hard. It was ridiculous to dredge up all this stuff about Meg and Doc. It was even more ridiculous to be thirty years old and still a crybaby.

"I don't know what's wrong with me," she said at last. "All this stuff with Babe and Old

Grandaddy's gotten worse in the hospital and I can't get in touch with Meg."

Doc found himself sitting up very alertly at the mention of Meg's name. Trying to sound casual, he asked, "Is Meggy coming home?"

"Who knows? She hasn't called me."

"She still living in California?"

"Yes," Lenny said, "in Hollywood."

Doc nodded. "Well, give me a call if she gets in. I'd like to see her."

Lenny looked Doc keenly in the eyes. "Oh, you would, huh?"

Doc met her gaze. "Yeah, Lenny, sad to say, but I would."

The two continued to stare at one another a few moments more. Then Doc glanced away and began slowly walking toward his pickup truck. As he sat down behind the wheel he looked back at Lenny. She was still standing in the shadow of the mimosa tree, sadly clutching her sack of pecans.

Two

The Greyhound bus heading slowly toward Hazlehurst was full of the kind of tired-out country people who don't smile, partly because they have lost all their hope and partly because they have lost all their teeth. The bus's dusty, imitation-leather seats were covered with life's sorriest specimens: milky-eyed, stringy-haired unwed mothers with milky-eyed, stringy-haired children whining on their laps; shriveled old black men heading back home with their savings hidden in their socks so they could buy a pine box and die "where da air don' stink"; and the usual collection of strange souls whose various physical and mental diseases kept the other passengers awake, if not alert.

Only one person on the bus still seemed to have the ghost of a dream left in her heart. Meg Magrath, maybe too skinny and sad looking to be truly beautiful, but also too full of some peculiar longing to be counted among the damned, didn't resemble her fellow passengers. Her white-blond hair, though it blew frayed and frazzled in the hot wind of an open window, obviously hadn't been cut with a bowl for a guide; and her clothes, though oddly whimsical and wrinkled, obviously hadn't been bought in a farm store. But what made Meg stand apart from the others on the bus wasn't just her looks and her clothing. There was something of the caged cat in the way she held herself. Other people on the bus sat like numbed lambs bound for slaughter, but not Meg. Her long legs tossed over a large tote bag, she smoked cigarette after cigarette with a kind of determined intensity, and as she stared out a window her dark eyes flashed with strange anger—strange because the anger seemed to be directed more at herself than at the world, as though she had let the universe down somehow but was too proud to apologize.

An ancient billboard outside Meg's window proclaimed: YOU'LL LOVE HAZLEHURST. Meg laughed at its words and thought, You betcha. You'll love Hazlehurst about as much as you'll love being boiled in oil.

The bus made a lazy turn down a road that led into Hazlehurst's poorest section. Several of the passengers began to get ready to depart; this was their part of town.

A plain-faced woman in her sixties who was dressed in faded overalls turned to her washed-out daughter and pointed to Meg. Eyeing a paper rose perched on top a rather unusual velvet beret Meg wore, she asked, "Is that the other sister?"

The daughter nodded glumly. "Yes. The one that moved to Hollywood."

Meg heard the women but didn't look at them. Instead she opened a bottle of Empirin and tossed a few of the aspirin tablets into her mouth. Then, sucking the Empirin like candy, she watched a group of black children standing outside the bus feeding tin cans and dirty paper to some goats. Oh yeah, she thought. How you *will* love Hazlehurst.

It was the middle of the afternoon. The sun was shining hard on Hazlehurst's saddest section. Meg's throat tightened as she looked out on the dilapidated houses set on bricks, splintered houses with white paint worn so thin she could see the gray of the wood underneath.

As a child, Meg had taken secret, solitary bike rides along these forlorn streets. She had watched kids her own age sitting inside the bleak houses and had eyed those children as mercilessly as children in her part of town eyed her—maybe even more mercilessly. She had stared straight at the children until they had gotten scared and run away.

The bus passed a trashed-out auto garage littered with broken car parts and moss-covered mechanical remains. Meg looked at the garage the way she had once looked at the poor children. Then she turned away from the window and thrust her bottle of Empirin against her tight, sore heart.

Once when she'd just moved to Hollywood and was certain stardom waited around the corner, Meg had seen a book called *You Can't Go Home Again* in a store. The title had made her grin with pleasure. Good, she had thought, 'cause I don't want to go home ever again. Now, older and no longer waiting for stardom,

Meg knew the truth behind the book's title. It's not that home doesn't draw you back over and over, it's just that what it draws you back to is heartbreaking.

At last, the bus made its way to the town square. Meg glanced once more out the window at a red brick post office and a yellow brick courthouse. Two black men sitting on green lawn chairs outside the courthouse waved at the bus riders. No one waved back.

The bus rolled by a boarded-up movie theater and Meg reached for her tote bag. She was almost home, like it or not.

Lenny had sent her an insistent, crazed telegram hinting at bullet holes, death, and other horrors. At first Meg tried to ignore the ravings on the paper by telling herself that Lenny always overreacted, but at last Lenny's pleas for help had gotten to her and she stormed the bus station in Los Angeles and began her journey back to Hazlehurst.

Lordy, Lordy, Meg thought as the bus went by a granite statue of a Confederate soldier, I'm like Dorothy returning home at the end of *The Wizard of Oz.* Only thing is, if I could make my wishes come true by clicking my heels three times, I'd be on my way to Oz instead.

Meanwhile, in the kitchen of the Magrath home, Lenny was trying to make her own wishes come true by striking a match to her birthday candle and letting the wax drippings form a pool at the center of her cookie. Ever since Doc Porter had driven off in the morning, she had been wandering about in tears. At last, she had happened to put her hands in the pockets of her sweater and had discovered her cookie and candle. Wiping away the tears, she had decided to make one more attempt to stand the candle on the cookie. It seemed a better thing to do than crying about Billy Boy and everything else.

The afternoon sun was streaming on Lenny's back, turning her hair into an angel's halo. She brushed a strand away from her face and waited anxiously for the wax to harden a little. Then, desperately, she shoved the candle into the wax.

It didn't fall!

Lenny eyed the candle for a moment, sort of stunned that she had succeeded at something on this most gloomy of days. Finally, breathlessly, she began to sing:

Happy birthday to me,
Happy birthday to me,
Happy birthday, dear Lenny,
Happy birthday to me.

She closed her eyes tightly and inhaled. I wish, she thought, oh how I wish, I wish, I wish . . . But what exactly, specifically, should she wish for? For Old Grandaddy to be released from all his agony? For everything with Babe to turn out to be a terrible nightmare? For Meg to come home and help out with all the trouble? For a husband? A new job? A new life? A new horse? There were so many wishes in Lenny's heart.

At last, she decided to give her wish to Old Grandaddy. Then she opened her eyes and blew out her candle.

Now what to do?

Lenny stared around the kitchen. A helpless feeling gripped her. Chick had told her to stay put and wait for Meg's call. But hours had passed and still the phone hadn't rung once. And even though Lenny knew Chick was taking care of things with Babe over at the jail, she felt nervous about just sitting around doing nothing. Then, glancing at her still-smoking birthday candle, she thought, What a shame that a person can't have a birthday wish for every year of her life. I could really use a lot more wishes.

She picked up a match. Maybe it would be okay if she lit her candle just one more time and made another, teeny-weeny wish?

An hour later, as Lenny lit her thirtieth match and prepared to make her thirtieth birthday wish, she heard a familiar whistle in the distance followed by a whooping shout: "I'm home! Anybody home?"

Her heart pounding with sudden joy, Lenny leaped from her chair. "Meg?"

Meg stood at a latched screen door at the front of the house wiping the grime from the bus ride off her face. She was hot and tired and aching from the weight of the tote bag on her shoulder, but when she saw Lenny racing toward her from the kitchen hallway, she was suddenly happy and her eyes lit up.

"Lenny!"

"Meg!"

Lenny ran through the living room, her own eyes flooded with relief. Meg, grinning through the screen, looked so at ease, so confident. And still—Lenny had to admit—so gorgeous.

Lenny unlatched the door and the two sisters, who had so often in the past fought like dogs, fell into each other's arms with joy.

"Well Meg!"

"Oh Lenny!"

"Why Meg!"

"Why Lenny!"

Lenny clung to her sister's back. She was surprised by a skinniness in Meg's bones. Had Meg always been this thin or had Lenny just gotten fat? When she thought of Meg, it was of someone tough and powerful, with lean, taut muscles, but the body she was now holding was fragile and even trembling. "Oh Meggy! Why didn't you call? Did you fly in? You didn't take a bus, did you?"

But Meg couldn't answer any of her sister's questions. She was taking in the warmth of Lenny's body againt hers, and she was looking with amazement at the safe, gentle living room of her childhood. Nothing was any different—the same smell of Pledge wax, the same sofa where she had sprawled and dreamed, the same clock ticking noisy and regular. Why had she stayed away from home all these years since high school? And why had she been irked about coming back? Why, it was great to be home, and even greater to be in Lenny's arms. Obviously, the tension that had always existed between the two of them had been merely a part of childhood. Now that they were adults, they could put the past behind them and express all the love in their hearts. Or so Meg thought.

Meg's eyes went watery with tears she didn't want her sister to see, and she whispered, "Dear Lenny."

It was amazing to be in this room again, as if all the years Meg had been away weren't real and she was still the most popular girl at Hazlehurst High, the girl everybody knew was going to take Hollywood by storm and wind up with one of those fancy-schmancy movie star homes with a heart-shaped swimming pool. Life had seemed so full of promise when she had last stood here.

"Why didn't you give us a call?" Lenny was asking.

Something in Lenny's tone—a certain whininess that had always bothered Meg—brought Meg back to the present. She blinked her eyes into control and pulled back from the embrace. She could see dark circles under Lenny's eyes and worry lines around her mouth and forehead. So time hadn't stood still in Hazlehurst, after all. And maybe the reunion with Lenny wasn't going to be exactly as easy as Meg had first hoped.

"My God," Meg laughed, staring at Lenny's deepest wrinkles. "We're getting so old!"

Lenny's mouth dropped again. She felt a shock of pain and wanted to cry out in protest at Meg's words, but Meg went on: "Oh I called. Of course I called."

Lenny decided to ignore the comment about aging. She, too, wanted to put all fighting into the past. "Well, I never talked to you."

Meg shrugged and tossed her tote bag onto

the floor. "I know. I let the phong ring right off the hook."

"Well, I was out most of the morning seeing to Babe," Lenny said, picking up the tote bag and beginning to carry it toward the dining room.

"Yeah?" Meg asked, following Lenny. "So what is all this business about Babe? How could you send me such a telegram about Babe? And Zackery! You say somebody's shot Zackery?"

Lenny nodded with gravity. "Yes, they have."

"Well good Lord. Is he dead?"

"No. But he's in the hospital. He was shot in the stomach."

Meg felt her own stomach and grimaced. "In his stomach! How awful! Do they know who shot him?"

Lenny nodded and sat down at the dining-room table.

"Well, who?" Meg asked.

Lenny didn't say anything, but Meg saw that she knew who the assailant was. "Who was it?" Still no response from Lenny. Finally, Meg took her sister by the arm. "Who? *Who?*"

Looking up at Meg with helpless tears, Lenny shouted, "*Babe!* They're all saying Babe shot him! They took her to jail! It's horrible! It's awful!"

Meg stood dumbstruck for a moment. Babe, the youngest of the sisters, was also the sweetest. Babe never even fought with people. It was utterly impossible for Meg to believe that her pretty, baby-faced little sister would ever yell at her husband, much less try to kill him. "Jail! Good Lord, *jail*! Well, who? Who's saying it? Who?!"

Lenny took a deep breath. Then: "Everyone! The policeman, the sheriff, Zackery . . ." And in a whisper: "Even Babe's saying it. Even Babe herself."

Meg shook her head with disbelief. "Well for God's sake. For God's sake."

Lenny, hysterical now, burst into sobs. "Oh it's horrible. It's horrible. It's just *horrible*!"

It sure as hell is, Meg thought, but knew such words might give Lenny cardiac arrest. Instead she said, "Now, calm down, Lenny. Just calm down. Would you like a Coke?"

Lenny couldn't stop crying.

"Here," Meg said, rushing to the kitchen, "I'll get you a Coke."

Meg yanked a Coke from the refrigerator, started back with it to the dining room, then stopped and took a huge swig from the bottle before returning to her sister.

Lenny was staring into space catatonically when Meg handed her the Coke but seemed to come alive again when she felt the cold bottle in her fingers.

"Why?" Meg asked Lenny, sitting down beside her at the table. "Why would she shoot him? *Why?*"

Lenny grimaced. What she was about to say scared her more than anything, but Meg had to know: "Oh I hate to say this . . . I do hate to say this . . . but I believe Babe is ill. I mean in-her-head ill."

Meg wouldn't hear of it. "Oh now, Lenny, don't you say that! There're plenty of good sane reasons to shoot another person and I'm sure that Babe had one."

Lenny glanced at Meg as though to say, "You really believe that?"

Meg—who didn't actually believe that—hurried on. "Now what we've got to do is get her the best lawyer in town. Do you have any ideas on who's the best lawyer in town?"

Again, Lenny began to sob. "Well, Zackery is, of course, but he's been shot!"

Meg slid down wearily in her chair. "Well, count him out. Just count him and his whole firm out."

Wiping the tears away from her face, Lenny nodded. "Anyway, you don't have to worry, she's already got a lawyer."

"She does? Who?"

"Barnette Lloyd," Lenny said, but Meg gave her a blank stare. "Annie Lloyd's boy. He just opened his office and Uncle Watson said we'd be doing Annie a favor by hiring him up."

Meg rolled her eyes. Fat, old Uncle Watson was just a few steps above his daughter Chick as far as Meg was concerned, and Chick was a step above nothing. It annoyed Meg that Lenny was always trying to please everybody, always trying to apologize somehow for having been born. "Doing Annie a favor? Well what about Babe? Do we want to do her a favor of thirty or forty years in jail? Have you thought about that?"

Lenny cringed and slumped her shoulders even lower. Meg was always finding fault with her, shouting at her. "Now don't snap at me," Lenny began, knowing her voice was starting to whine and how Meg hated it. "I try to do what's right."

Meg snorted. Here she was, only home five minutes, and already Lenny was going into her martyr-of-the-earth routine.

Feeling Meg's judgment and exasperation, Lenny fled from the table. Meg watched her hurry over to a sideboard and pick up a set of towels. Oh and now she's going to be an even bigger martyr and start cleaning the house while Babe rots in jail, Meg thought. Out loud she said, "Well boo hoo, hoo, hoo."

Not looking at Meg, Lenny began running up to the second floor of the house with the towels. Meg grabbed her tote bag and followed. The two sisters banged up the steps, as furious with each other as they had ever been as children and teenagers.

At the top of the steps, Lenny spun around. "And what was that you said about how old we're getting? Only you didn't mean *we*, you meant *me*, didn't you? My face is getting all pinched up and my hair is falling out in the comb."

Scared about Babe and irritated by Lenny, Meg was about to shoot back a smart remark as to how Lenny worked at looking old and dowdy and pathetic when suddenly she remembered what the day's date was, and her face softened. "Why Lenny! It's your birthday, May thirty-first. How could I forget. Happy birthday."

The two sisters' eyes met and they both started to smile. Maybe Meg could find a way to stop feeling angry and guilty every time Lenny opened her mouth. Maybe Lenny could find a way to stop feeling jealous and hurt every time Meg opened her mouth. Maybe they could get through this Babe crisis without tearing each other's eyes out, without screaming or fighting or dredging up all their old wounds.

Then, realizing that Lenny was thirty, Meg shook her head and again said, "My God, we're getting so old," and Lenny's face went tight and strained all over again. Not that Meg noticed, though. No sooner had she repeated her cruel remark about aging than she loped off down the hallway toward Old Grandaddy's room. "Is Old Grandaddy here?" she whispered.

Lenny eyed Meg as though her sister had lost her mind. "Why no. Old Grandaddy's at the hospital."

Meg looked a little surprised, a little relieved. Old Grandaddy, although supposedly Meg's biggest fan and supporter, was always making Meg feel like the world's biggest failure. Maybe it was the way that he seemed to demand success from Meg, or at least expect it. It never occurred to Old Grandaddy that Meg wouldn't make it big with her singing career. His letters made her blood pressure rise: *How come you don't call up that there Johnny Carson and get yourself on his TV show? I'd surely enjoy seeing you on my television, Meggy.* Still, it was too bad his health was causing him troubles, and Meg felt a little guilty about being glad he was back in the hospital. "Again?" she asked Lenny.

Lenny stared at Meg in stunned silence.

Meg appeared not to notice her sister's shock. She walked right by Lenny and opened the door to the sisters' bedroom.

"Meg!" Lenny shouted, following Meg into the room.

The bedroom was just as Meg remembered it, long and sunny and full of beds. There were double beds for Lenny and Meg, and a single bed for Babe. Meg eyed the beds and then the three bureaus and footlockers beside them. We grew up like little soldiers in here, she thought, then, noticing a frantic Lenny staring at her with shock, said, "What?"

"Don't you remember?" Lenny asked. "I wrote you about all those blood vessels popping in his brain!"

"Popping?" Meg asked.

"And how he was so anxious to hear from you and to find out about your singing career."

Meg closed her eyes a moment, then opened them and began searching through her tote bag for a cigarette, though what she actually needed was an enormous bottle full of bourbon.

"Didn't you get my letters?" Lenny asked.

Meg sighed and lit the cigarette. "Oh, I don't know, Lenny. To tell you the truth, sometimes I kinda don't read your letters."

"What?"

Meg blew a stream of smoke out the side of her mouth and shrugged. "I'm sorry. I used to read them. It's just, since Christmas, reading them gives me these slicing pains right here in my chest." And she indicated a spot just over her heart.

Lenny turned away. "I see," she began, trying hard not to let her hurt show. "I see. Is that why you didn't use that money Old Grandaddy sent you to come home Christmas? Because you hate us so much?"

Meg went over to Lenny. Taking her sister by the arms, she said, "Oh, Lenny. Do you think I'd be getting slicing pains in my chest if I didn't care about you? If I hated you? Honestly now, do you think I would?"

"No," Lenny said, not in the least taking comfort in Meg's words but wanting—as always—to avoid a fight.

At four o'clock in the afternoon, Chick called Lenny from the courthouse to say that bail had been set for Babe. Lenny was to come to the jail around five with a change of clothes so that Babe wouldn't have to leave her cell in the same bloodstained outfit she had worn upon her arrival. Lenny said how she had already gotten some things from the Botrelle home and would bring them. She didn't have the courage to add that she would also bring Meg.

Meg, showered and changed and bored, didn't feel like hanging around the house for another hour. Her initial delight at seeing that nothing in the home had changed had turned to frustration and restlessness. She wanted to head over to the jail right away and talk with Babe until it was time for her to be released. Maybe Babe would explain why she had decided to fill Zackery's stomach full of lead. Maybe there wouldn't be any need for a court trial once Babe told what had actually happened.

But Lenny didn't want to get to the jail early. There were forms to fill out, things that Babe had to do, she explained to Meg. The real truth was Lenny needed an hour to shore herself up for whatever fireworks were going to explode when Chick and Meg ran into each other.

So the sisters compromised and decided to first stop at a country store for some ice cream, Babe's favorite dessert.

Lenny unpacked Babe's white suitcase and selected a pink and white suit with a matching pink pocketbook that had a little jeweled poodle on the clasp.

Meg climbed into Lenny's car while Lenny carefully laid Babe's clothes out in the backseat, and then they were off. Lenny drove slowly and cautiously along curvy roads; Meg pushed down on an imaginary accelerator in hopes of making the car go faster. For a time, the sisters didn't speak. Each sat thinking about Babe. Lenny wondered if Babe had shot Zackery because she was crazy. Meg wondered if she had shot him because he was ugly.

At last Meg lit a cigarette and said, "So. Babe shot Zackery Botrelle, the richest and most powerful man in all of Hazlehurst, slap in the gut. It's hard to believe."

Lenny agreed as to how it most certainly was. "Little Babe . . . shooting off a gun."

"Little Babe," Meg echoed, picturing her little sister's big blue eyes and cherubic smile. Babe—though perhaps not the brightest of the three sisters—was certainly the nicest. Both Meg and Lenny had always been very protective toward her, enjoyed braiding her hair when she was little and buying her things with their allowance money.

Lenny suddenly smiled. "Do you remember how Old Grandaddy used to call her his Dancing Sugar Plum? Why, he was so proud and happy the day she finally married Zackery."

Meg's eyes darkened at the memory of pretty, innocent Babe walking down the aisle with slovenly, foul-breathed Zackery. Old Grandaddy, thrilled to have married one of his grandchildren off to the richest man in town, had to be restrained from cheering out loud when she had said "I do." "Yes, I remember," Meg allowed, taking a deep drag on her cigarette. "It was his finest hour."

Not catching her sister's irony, Lenny smiled again. "He remarked how Babe was gonna skyrocket right to the heights of Hazlehurst society."

"Oh Lordy, Lordy," Meg said. "And what does Old Grandaddy say now?"

Lenny pulled her car up to a small country store. A little embarrassed, she said, "Well, I haven't had the courage to tell him all about this as yet."

Meg leaped from the car before Lenny barely had a chance to park. Lenny's snail-pace driving combined with the mention of Old Grandaddy made her feel like moving fast and free. She glanced past the store to the road ahead and thought how nice it would be to bolt down the road and never look back. But instead she turned into the store and walked directly to the freezer.

By the time Lenny caught up with her, Meg had already taken a Nutty Buddy ice cream from the bin and was ripping off its paper.

"Brother," Meg said, "I know Old Grandaddy's gonna go on about my singing career when I see him. Just like he always does."

Lenny watched Meg toss her Nutty Buddy wrapper to the floor. Probably, Lenny supposed, Meg wouldn't even bother to pay for the ice cream if Lenny weren't around. "Well, how is your career going?" Lenny asked.

Meg glanced away. "It's not."

Lenny opened up the freezer bin and reached for a carton of chocolate swirl ice cream, Babe's absolute favorite. "Why? Aren't you still singing at that club down on Malibu Beach?"

"No," Meg said cheerfully, leaving the open freezer bin to explore the other aisles. "I'm not singing. I'm not singing at all."

Something in Meg's tone made Lenny feel nervous. She watched her sister a moment, then picked up the Nutty Buddy wrapper, closed the freezer, and followed after her. A little anxiously, she asked, "Well, what do you do then?"

Meg smiled. "What I do is pay cold storage bills for a dog food company. That's what I do."

"Gosh," Lenny said, feeling even more anxious, but wanting to be helpful. "Don't you think it would be a good idea to stay in the show business field?"

"Oh, maybe."

"Like Old Grandaddy says, 'With your talent all you need is exposure. Then you can make your own breaks!' "

Meg stared at Lenny but said nothing.

Lenny went on: "Did you hear his suggestion

about getting your foot in one of those blocks of cement they've got out there?"

"Yeah," Meg said quietly. "I think I've heard that. And I'll probably hear it again." Then, calling out to a clerk at the front of the store: "*Hey!* Do you have anything to drink around here . . . to the tune of straight bourbon?"

The clerk looked at Meg as though she had asked him if he sold dead babies. "No," he said somberly, "there's no liquor."

"Hell," Meg said, and walked off to another aisle. Lenny followed on her heels so that Meg could almost feel her breathing. For a moment Meg felt like spinning around and screaming at Lenny to stop bugging her, stop following her, stop asking her questions. Stop—in a way—loving her. But then she turned and saw that Lenny was looking at her with such confusion and tenderness that Meg felt embarrassed for having wanted to scream at her. So she pointed to a barrel near Lenny instead. "What's this?" she asked. "Pecans? Great, I love pecans."

She dove for the barrel, yanked the two largest pecans she could find from it, and tried to crack them open by smashing them against one another. "Come on," she said, "crack, you demons!"

Lenny shook her head. "They *have* a nutcracker."

"Ah, what's the sport in a nutcracker?" Meg asked, gnawing at the hard shells of the pecans with her teeth. "Where's the challenge?"

Lenny lifted the nutcracker and offered it to Meg, but Meg ignored it and stamped the pecans open on the floor. "There!" she shouted as the pecans splattered across the shop. Then she bent down and began hunting the floor for the meats of her nuts. "Mmm," she said at last. "Delicious! Let's get us some fresh pecans."

"We don't need any pecans," Lenny told her, more than a little upset by the fact that her sister was eating off the floor. "Doc Porter brought us a whole sack over."

Meg started suddenly when she heard Doc's name and glanced up at Lenny, but Lenny was walking away, heading for the checkout counter with her ice cream carton and Meg's Nutty Buddy wrapper.

The clerk rang up Lenny's bill with some distaste. Lenny knew he was angry about the pecan shells on his floor and the gooey ice cram wrapper on his counter. It bothered her that Meg didn't seem to care what people thought, and it bothered her that she herself had to care so much.

Meg approached the register, her expression faraway and dreamy. She stood quietly by Lenny's side a moment, then said, "Doc. Gosh . . . the last I heard of Doc, he was up in the East painting houses to make a living. Heard he was living with some Yankee woman who made clay pots."

"Joan," Lenny said firmly.

"What?"

"Her name's Joan. She came down here with him. She gave me one of her pots."

Meg stared at Lenny. Lenny began to scrounge through her change purse for the money to pay the clerk, then smiled at Meg and said, as matter-of-factly as she could, "Doc's married to her."

Meg's eyes widened. "Married . . ."

"Uh-huh." And with that, Lenny picked up her items and walked briskly from the store.

This time it was Meg who was walking slowly. She followed Lenny out to the car in a hazy stupor. "Doc married a Yankee?"

"That's right," Lenny said, her voice sounding rather cheerful, "and they have two kids."

"Kids . . ." Meg echoed with horror.

"A boy and a girl."

Lenny got into the car and started the engine. Meg lingered outside a few moments, her face ashen and befuddled. Married? Doc? To a Yankee? And a father? It all seemed incredibly surreal.

Meg opened the passenger door and dropped into her seat with a thud. "God," she whispered, "then his kids must be half Yankee."

"I suppose," Lenny said in a pleasant, singsong tone.

Meg sat in hopeless shock as Lenny drove along cheerily. Somehow she had expected Doc to go to his grave still in love with her. The thought that he no longer slept with her yearbook picture under his pillow mortified her. Not that she had ever slept with his picture under her pillow, nor that she had ever truly given much thought to him over the years. But that he should go and get married. To a *Yankee.* And have half-Yankee children . . . "God," she finally said, her voice lost and hoarse, "that really gets me. I don't know why, but that *really* gets me."

Lenny arched her eyebrows primly. "I don't know why it should."

Meg turned to Lenny. She was about to let hurl some comment about Lenny always having been jealous not only of Doc but of all Meg's other boyfriends as well when suddenly something caught her eye that made her forget about her quarrels with Lenny and her feelings for Doc. For looming straight ahead was the jail.

Three

The inside of the jail was bleak and dark. Lenny stood in the waiting room running her hands back and forth across her purse handle to keep them from trembling as she waited for Babe to be sprung from her cell. Meg, on the other hand, seemed to be enjoying herself in a strange way. She ran from corner to corner of the room, trying to find a good hiding place so she could surprise Babe with her presence.

So far Chick and Meg hadn't spoken a word to each other. Chick stood near her father, Uncle Watson, as he finished up business at the captain's desk, and pretended that Meg was invisible.

Lenny glanced from Chick to Meg warily, then turned her gaze to a long, dark corridor. How she longed to hear Babe's tap-tap-tapping high heels approach, but when she finally did, she thought she was imagining things and didn't believe her ears until she heard Babe shouting, "Lenny! I'm free! I'm free!"

Babe burst into the room waving her pink pocketbook with exuberance. She was an angelic-looking young woman with long, reddish-blond curls and cornflower-blue eyes. And though she was only twenty-four years old, she looked even younger than that with her endless freckles and soft, innocent smile. Anyone seeing her would have guessed her to be a high school student out on vacation, not a dangerous prisoner out on bail.

"Take me home!" Babe cried out. "I wanna go home!"

Lenny rushed to her little sister. "Oh Babe, you're going home. We'll go home."

Suddenly Meg jumped out from behind a post. Babe screamed with delight and amazement and all three of the sisters flung their arms around each other. "Oh Meg!" Babe said. "Look, it's Meg."

From across the room, Chick watched the sisters out of the corner of her eyes. Any demonstration of affection had a way of getting on Chick's nerves, but especially demonstrations of affection that involved Meg.

The sisters headed eagerly toward the jailhouse door. "Oh it's so good to see you," Babe told Meg. "I'm so glad you're home. I'm so relieved."

Meg squeezed Babe's hand hard. There was no one on earth who could open Meg's heart the way Babe could. Sweet Babe, like a puppy, approached those she loved with so much warmth and goodness that it was impossible not to want to hold her. Old Grandaddy had always said that the world would always be kind to her because she was so kind to the world.

Babe opened the door and squinted her eyes at the daylight, then took in a deep breath of fresh air, spun around in a circle, and tossed her purse in the sky. Meg watched her with both pleasure and puzzlement. Babe seemed so much herself, so happy and youthful and alive. How could she have shot someone? It was inconceivable to Meg that such a thing could have happened. And yet, if Meg were able to see Babe clearly, she would have noticed that her sister was no longer the naive teenager she had once been, and that behind the Barbie doll looks and the puppydog charm was a person whose eyes burned fierce and volatile.

A large crowd of people had gathered around the jail so they could someday tell their grandchildren that they had personally witnessed the emergence of Babe Botrelle from her prison cell. Their gawking expressions made Lenny feel like a zoo exhibit and she tried her best to hurry Babe along to the car, but Babe didn't seem to mind all the prying eyes and laughed with pleasure at the sight of so many people.

Soon Uncle Watson caught up with the sisters. He was a plump, jolly sort of man who loved cookies and candy the way other men loved money and women. Now, not yet having had a chance to talk with Meg, he ambled to her side. "Why, hello Margaret," he said. "You're looking mighty good. It's good to see you."

Meg grinned. "Thank you, Uncle Watson. And how have you been?"

"Oh, not bad for an old, tired, fat man."

Babe winked at Meg. "Uncle Watson thinks he's fat."

"He *is* fat," Chick called out, scurrying up to her father's side.

Meg spun around and looked at Chick with feigned surprise. "Why Chick! Hello!"

Chick flared her nostrils as though she had just caught a whiff of something foul and green in her refrigerator. "Hello, Cousin Margaret," she purred. "And what brings you back to Hazlehurst?"

"Oh I came on home," Meg said casually. "I came on home to see about Babe."

Babe smiled at Meg gratefully as the three sisters squeezed into the front seat of Lenny's car, leaving Chick to sputter and flail at her father on the sidewalk.

Meg was worried. The whole way home from the jail, Babe had chattered away happily about how pretty the day was, how nice Meg looked, how sweet Lenny was to have brought her some clothes to wear home, and how good Uncle Watson was to have put up her bail money. But not one word about the shooting of Zackery. And now, back home in the Magrath kitchen, Babe was perched atop a counter, merrily eating the chocolate swirl ice cream Lenny had gotten for her and debating the pros and cons of mashing ice cream into soup before eating it.

Uncle Watson and Chick had followed the sisters home in Chick's car and now were standing in the kitchen alongside Lenny and Meg. For the longest time everyone—including Chick—kept quiet and let Babe talk about ice cream. But at last Meg interrupted: "So, how *are* things with you, Babe?"

Chick, driven to the point of no return by Babe's chatter, pounced on Meg's question. "Well, they are *dismal* if you want my opinion. She is refusing to cooperate with her lawyer, that nice-looking young Lloyd boy. She won't tell any of us why she committed this heinous crime."

Babe flashed a look at Chick, then tossed her ice cream carton aside and hopped off the counter. "Oh look!" she cried out. "Lenny brought my suitcase from home! And my saxophone! Thank you!" And she ran toward the saxophone with glee.

Chick walked over to her. "Now that young lawyer expects to get some concrete answers!"

Babe didn't glance up at Chick. Instead, lifting the saxophone from its case and cradling it in her arms like a baby, she turned to Meg and smiled. "Come look at my saxophone, Meg. I went to Jackson and bought it used."

Chick decided to speak a little louder: *"No more of this nonsense and stubbornness from you—"*

"Feel it," Babe said to Meg, handing her the saxophone. "It's so heavy."

Meg took the instrument into her arms as Chick leaned toward Babe's ear: *"—or they'll put you in jail and throw away the key!"*

The room went silent.

Meg stared at the saxophone; Lenny looked at the floor; Babe eyed her own feet; and Chick licked her lips like a cat that had just finished a bowl of milk. Only Uncle Watson seemed oblivious to the tension that had made its way into the room. He was moving toward Lenny's cookie bin as though he were a man possessed.

At last Chick turned to her father for confirmation. "Isn't that right, Daddy? Won't they throw away the key?"

Uncle Watson stealthily slid one of his pudgy hands into the cookie bin. "Well, honey," he said amicably, trying to keep Chick from seeing what he was doing, "I don't know about that."

Chick shook her head with exasperation and refocused her attention on Babe. "Well they will," she informed her cousin. "And leave you there to rot." And then, smiling sweetly, as though she had only Babe's best interests at heart: "So Rebecca, what are you going to tell Mr. Lloyd about shooting Zackery? What are your reasons going to be?"

Taking her saxophone back from Meg, Babe stared directly into Chick's eyes with anger so intense even Chick began to feel scared. "That I didn't like his looks," she said. "I just didn't like his stinking looks! And I don't like yours much either, Chick-the-Stick! So leave me alone! I mean it! Leave me alone!" And then, racing from the room with her saxophone: *"Ooooooooh!"*

Again, everyone became extremely quiet. This time even Uncle Watson, his mouth full of cookies, looked concerned.

Chick eyed Uncle Watson's full mouth gloomily. It unnerved her that he wasn't leaping to her defense. If she were the father and he were the daughter, she would be chasing Babe with a stick of fire right now.

At last Chick realized no one was going to help her but herself. "Well," she began kindly, "I was only trying to warn her that she's going to have to help herself. It's just that she doesn't understand how serious the situation is, does she? She doesn't have the vaguest idea."

"Well," Lenny said, "it's true she does seem a little confused."

Chick snorted. "And that's putting it mildly, Lenny honey. That's putting it mighty mild."

Meg began searching for a cigarette. It was either smoke or spit at Chick, and if she started spitting at Chick, she might never stop. That Chick should voice doubts about Babe's sanity out loud was too much, especially because Meg shared all those doubts down deep.

Chick caught the hostility in Meg and decided to make the most of it. Grinning at her, she said, "So, Margaret, how's your singing career going?"

Meg found a cigarette and began hunting for a match.

Chick leaned close to Meg and raised her brows with feigned innocence. "We keep looking for your picture in the movie magazines."

Meg struck a match as hard as she could and stared at Chick blankly.

"You know," Chick said, "you shouldn't smoke. It causes cancer of the lungs. They say each cigarette is just a little death stick."

Meg blew smoke from her mouth with relish. "That's what I like about it, Chick—taking a drag off of death." And, after inhaling longer and deeper than she had in her life: "Mmm! What power! What exhilaration! Want a drag?"

Lenny watched the two women with fear. She had once seen Chick and Meg on top of a school jungle gym ripping each other's hair out after Chick had called Meg the daughter of a crazy lady. Memories of how happy Meg had been pulling hunks of Chick's yellow curls from her head returned to Lenny and she quickly said, "Oh, did I tell y'all that Zackery's liver's been saved? His sister, she told me his liver was saved. Isn't that good news?"

But Lenny's tension-breaking ploy didn't work. Chick's and Meg's faces were still masks of hatred after she had finished speaking. So Lenny turned to Uncle Watson for help. He, in turn, swallowed another mouthful of cookies, then went over to Chick and Meg. "Well, yes," he said, wishing he had a nice cold glass of milk to wash his cookies down. "That's fine news. Mighty fine news. Did you hear all that news about the liver, Little Chicken?"

Chick gritted her teeth at the use of her much-despised childhood nickname. "I heard it," she said.

Meg leaned toward Chick and began to flap her arms like a chicken. "Cluck," she whispered.

"And don't call me Chicken," Chick said to Uncle Watson, her teeth gritting up even tighter.

"Cluck, cluck, cluck," Meg said.

Chick kept her attention on her father, but her words were obviously intended for Meg's ears. "If I've told you once I've told you a hundred times not to call me Chicken."

Now Meg launched into an elaborate chicken-in-a-barnyard imitation—an imitation she had made famous back in school when she would run into Chick at recess. Poking her head this way and that, she let her noises get louder: "Cluck, cluck, cluck . . ."

Chick's eyes filled with furious tears as she wagged an about-to-have-a-tantrum finger at her father's face: "I'm not twelve years old anymore!"

"Cluck!"

Chick spun around to Meg. For a moment she looked as though she was about to push her fingers through her cousin's eyes. Then, perhaps deciding that such an act wouldn't sit well with the members of the Ladies' Social League, she raced out of the house, slamming the door behind her.

Night had come to Hazlehurst. From the rickety, second-floor terrace of the Magrath house where Meg and Babe sat, Meg could see a full moon glowing in the sky.

A long time back, when Meg had lived in Biloxi, she had sung at a tiny nightclub called Greeny's. Doc had come from Tulane University to hear her every night. He'd sit alone at a table, his eyes full of pride when she'd walk out on stage. Then, after her set, the two of them would get in his car and drive nowhere in particular. "You and me and the moon for our map," Doc would say. They would follow the moon down bumpy country roads while Meg sang songs to the night air.

Now, as Babe sat winding her freshly washed hair into big, pink sponge rollers, Meg lit a cigarette and thought back on her moony nights with Doc. What a nice voice I used to have, she thought, what a nice boy I used to kiss, what a nice girl I used to be . . .

Suddenly, a shrill screech from Chick's house caused Meg to forget her reveries and Babe to drop one of her rollers. Chick was shouting at her kids. The words came to Meg's and Babe's ears as clearly as if Chick were standing a foot away: "I said to get to bed now or I'll send you both to reform school! How would you like that?"

They'd probably love it, Meg thought. At least

it would get them away from their witch of a mother.

Babe smiled at Meg and said, "You know, Chick's hated us ever since we had to move here from Vicksburg to live with Old Grandmama and Old Grandaddy."

Meg shrugged. "She's an idiot."

"Yeah. Do you know what she told me this morning when I was still behind bars and couldn't get away from her?"

"What?"

"She told me how embarrassing it was for her all those years ago, you know, when Mama . . ."

Babe's voice faltered and broke off. She and Meg eyed each other a moment in silence, then Meg quietly said, "Yeah. Down in the cellar."

Babe nodded solemnly. "She said our mama had shamed the entire family and we were known notoriously all through Hazlehurst. Then she went on to say how I would be getting just as much bad publicity and humiliating her and the family all over again."

Meg felt a sorrow starting to fill her. "Ah, forget it Babe. Just forget it."

But Babe couldn't forget it. Leaning up close to Meg, she said, "I told her, 'Mama got *national* coverage! *National!*' And if Zackery wasn't a senator from Copiah County, I probably wouldn't even be getting statewide."

Meg reached for Babe's hand. "Of course you wouldn't."

Babe's innocent, cornflower-blue eyes searched Meg's sad, brown ones. "Gosh," she said after a moment. "Sometimes I wonder . . ."

"What?"

"Why she did it," Babe whispered. "Why Mama hung herself."

Meg immediately looked away from Babe. Talking about Mama was something she and Lenny just didn't do. Didn't even know how to do. But here was little Babe doing it. Meg stared at the moon for a time, then forced herself to turn back to Babe. Babe seemed to be waiting for Meg to tell her something. But I've got nothing for her, Meg thought.

"I don't know," Meg said at last. "She had a bad day. A real bad day."

"And that old yellow cat," Babe went on, her eyes getting wide, her voice tremulous. "It was sad about that old cat."

"Yeah," Meg said, wishing she had her Empirin bottle out on the terrace with her.

"I bet if Daddy hadn't've left us, they'd still be alive."

At the mention of her father, Meg thought, Forget the Empirin. Forget even bourbon. What I could use right now is a lobotomy. She had been her father's favorite, had reminded him of himself as a kid. And then he had walked out on her, on everyone. A shiftless, good-looking, good-time Charley. And I'm turning out to be just as bad as he was, she thought. Out loud she said, "Oh, I don't know."

Babe had a faraway look on her face. Her brow knitted up as though she was thinking hard about something. In a minute she said, " 'Cause it was after Daddy left that Mama started spending whole days just sitting there and smoking on the back porch steps."

"Yeah," Meg said, remembering how her

mother's eyes had seemed to get deader and deader each day, how her clothes had gotten too big for her, how her face had smiled less and less and then one day had stopped smiling altogether. "Well, I'm glad Daddy left . . . God he was such a bastard."

Babe, who had been too young to remember their father much, looked curiously at Meg. "I thought if she felt something for anyone it woulda been that old cat."

Meg shifted uncomfortably. If there was something she absolutely, positively did not want to think about, it was that cat. "Really," she told Babe, "with his white teeth, Daddy was such a bastard."

"Was he? I don't remember."

Meg blew a stream of cigarette smoke from her mouth and looked up at the moon again. Oh lady in the moon, she thought, here we are in Hazlehurst again. Only Old Grandaddy's become a sick man in the hospital, and Lenny's become a martyred spinster, and I've become a singer who can't sing, and Babe—here Meg looked at her sister sweetly rolling her hair into the sponge rollers—for some reason Babe's gone and become a would-be killer.

Meg sighed over the mess her family had become and inhaled deeply on her cigarette. It was spooky to realize that her whole family was failing miserably at life. And spookier still to know that all of this mess—every last bit of it—might have been prevented if it hadn't been for her mother and that damn yellow cat.

Four

Yellow and pink light flowed through the stained-glass windows of the Magrath house. It was early the next morning, a blue-sky day full of soft, southern breezes. The three sisters were in the kitchen. Babe was in seemingly high spirits as she removed piles of lemons from the refrigerator. She looked great: her hair was perfectly curled; the dress she wore was fresh, frilly, and feminine; and her face had the contented, blissful look of one who had slept peacefully. Lenny and Meg, on the other hand, looked depressed and haggard as they sat at the table pushing about bits of scrambled eggs. Each had lain awake in bed the night before watching Babe, who had tossed and turned and moaned with nightmares. Lenny had woken Babe once to ask what she was dreaming about, but Babe had denied dreaming anything.

How can she be like this? Lenny wondered as Babe cheerfully reached for a big canister of sugar so she could make herself some lemonade. It frightened Lenny that Babe could laugh and smile and act as if nothing was wrong when obviously everything was wrong.

Meg lifted a coffee cup and glanced at Lenny

as though to say, "You want to talk to her or should I?"

Lenny understood the meaning of Meg's look, but before she could respond, the sound of screaming, raging children burst through the windows of the kitchen. All three sisters looked out the screen door where they saw Chick and her kids coming out of their house. Peekay and Buck Jr. were purple-faced with fury as Chick yanked them toward her station wagon. "Do you want me to jerk both of you bald-headed?" she asked them.

Chick was even hotter in the face than her kids. As they smacked at her and each other, she attempted to get between them. With her hands on her hips, she made idle threats: "If you both don't shut up and get in this car, I'm gonna call up Santa Claus and tell him to come down the chimney and eat you both up!"

The kids paused in their screaming and smacking for a moment.

"I mean it!" Chick added.

Peekay and Buck Jr. obviously didn't believe her, though. No sooner were they in the car than they were starting up another battle.

Meg, Lenny, and Babe watched the station wagon pull down the driveway with intense relief, then Meg turned again to Lenny.

Lenny cleared her throat nervously. "Babe," she began delicately, "why won't you tell anyone about shooting Zackery?"

Babe reached into a silverware drawer, pulled out a big butcher knife, and let out a kind of frustrated moan.

"Why not?" Lenny asked again. "You must have had a good reason."

But Babe didn't say anything. Instead she turned to her lemons and began swatting at them with her huge knife.

Lenny swallowed. "Didn't you?"

Babe slashed the lemons in half. Finally, not looking at Lenny or Meg, she said, "I guess I did."

Lenny and Meg exchanged pleased glances. Now they were getting somewhere. "Well, what was it?" Lenny asked.

Babe lifted a lemon. For a time she seemed fascinated by some aspect of the fruit. She spun it around in her hand, then tightly gripped it in her palm like a good luck charm. She opened her mouth, seemed about to say something, then tossed the lemon back onto the counter, slashed it apart, and whispered, "I . . . I can't say."

"Why not?" Meg asked.

Babe stared at her slashed lemon. "Cause, I'm . . . sort of . . . protecting someone."

Lenny felt her heart leap with joy. "Oh Babe! Then you really didn't shoot him?!" And to the equally joyful Meg: "I *knew* she couldn't have done it! I knew it!"

Lenny and Meg grinned at each other and were about to begin a kind of happy, out-of-control-with-delight sort of dance when Babe spun around toward them with her butcher knife and said, "No, I shot him all right."

Lenny and Meg stopped grinning instantly.

"I meant to kill him," Babe went on, matter-of-factly. "I was aiming for his heart, but I guess my hands were shaking and I . . . just got him in the stomach. So, I'm guilty. And I'm just gonna have to take my punishment and go on to jail."

Meg nodded wearily. "I see."

As for Lenny, she sat paralyzed with lost hope. Tears filled her eyes as she pictured a lifetime of delivering chocolate chip cookies to a sister behind bars, and she sadly said, "Oh Babe . . ."

But Babe seemed to have resolved herself to her fate. Without a trace of sorrow, she continued making her lemonade. "Don't worry," she cheerfully told her sisters. "Jail's gonna be a relief for me. I can learn to play my saxophone. I won't have to live with Zackery anymore. And I won't have his snoopy old sister Lucille coming over and pushing me around."

Meg watched Babe pour lemonade into glasses. Something about Babe's saying jail would be a relief didn't make sense. What was it in Babe's life that was worse than being in prison? Granted, Zackery was disgusting, and Lucille was snoopy, but still . . .

"Here's your lemonade," Babe said, handing Meg a glass.

"Thanks."

"Taste okay?"

"Perfect."

Babe offered Lenny a glass but Lenny, still teary-eyed, shook her head. "I really don't feel very thirsty."

Shrugging, Babe carried the glass she had offered Lenny back to the counter. "Well, I like a lot of sugar in mine. I'm gonna add some more sugar."

Lenny and Meg watched as Babe added scoop

after scoop of sugar to her pitcher. Lenny noticed that the sugar was flying all over the counter, all over the floor. She tried to ignore the mess, but as more and more sugar started to pile up almost everywhere but in the pitcher, she found herself getting furious, and at last she couldn't take it anymore. "Oh now Babe, don't make such a mess here! And be careful with this sharp knife."

Babe looked at Lenny but said nothing. Instead she took a sip of her lemonade and then turned her attention to the kitchen window, where she watched the old rope swing blowing in the morning breeze. Blocking Lenny's irritation, she watched the swing move back and forth. Nice, Babe thought, nice and calm and gentle.

Lenny couldn't believe Babe wasn't cleaning up the sugar. Maybe Chick and Meg were the sort of people who expected you to clean up after them, but Babe? "Honestly now," she said, "all that sugar's going to make you sick!"

But Babe just kept looking at the swing and sipping her lemonade, so Lenny began to clean up the sugar herself. Each sweep of her dishcloth enraged her more and more. Why does she have to be this way? Lenny thought. Throwing sugar around. Staring out windows. Shooting her husband . . .

Suddenly, her heart pounding with frustration, Lenny ran to the corner of the kitchen where she kept her sun hat and gardening gloves. Without another word to Babe or Meg, she jammed the hat on her head, scooped up the gloves, and ran outside.

Babe kept staring out the window. In a moment, she could see Lenny, the green garden gloves now on her hands, rushing past the oak tree. "Boy," Babe said, "I don't know what's happening to Lenny."

Meg leaned back in her chair and lit a cigarette. "What do you mean?"

But Babe was watching Lenny too intensely to hear Meg's question. Now Lenny had passed the oak tree and was lumbering across the yard to the garden. Babe walked quickly to the screened-in porch that overlooked the garden so she could keep an eye on her sister.

For a moment, Meg sat alone at the kitchen table smoking, then she followed Babe out to the porch. Babe was sitting on a swinging sofa. Meg flopped down on a chair near her.

The porch was full of bright morning sun and comfortable white wicker furniture. It had always been one of Babe's favorite rooms in the house, maybe because the sofas and chairs were covered with pink, floral material.

Babe was peering out at Lenny, staring at her sister's green-gloved hands. Lenny was weeding, bending and straining, slump-shouldered, in a flower bed.

At last Babe shook her head and turned to Meg. "She's turning into Old Grandmama."

"You think so?"

"More and more. Look there."

Meg stared where Babe was pointing and watching Lenny a moment.

"See?" asked Babe. "She's even taken to wearing Old Grandmama's torn sun hat and her lime-green garden gloves. Lenny works out in the garden wearing the lime-green gloves of a dead woman."

Meg wrinkled her nose as Babe continued to stare at Lenny with morbid fascination. Babe had been just a little girl when Old Grandmama had died, but she still remembered the funeral, how Old Grandmama had looked so peculiar in a coffin with her cheeks all rouged up and her hands all covered with makeup. Old Grandaddy had wanted Babe to give her a kiss but Babe had refused. She didn't want to get near those strange, too-pink cheeks. And she didn't see how Lenny could stick her hands into those gloves. Anything dead made Babe want to scream. Especially dead cats.

Meg got up and walked into the kitchen for something more to eat. There she found a partially wrapped box of candy with a card. She picked up the card, and read it: HAPPY BIRTHDAY TO LENNY FROM THE BUCK BOYLES. The words felt like a slap to Meg. Chick had remembered Lenny's birthday with a present and Meg hadn't. Sighing, Meg grabbed the card and the box and walked back to Babe.

Babe looked at the card, puzzled a moment, then flung her hands across her face. "Oh no! Yesterday was Lenny's birthday!"

Nodding miserably, Meg recalled the smart remarks she had made to Lenny about getting old. "That's right," she said sadly.

Babe looked stricken. "Gosh, I forgot all about it."

"I know. I did too." And then, noticing the plastic wrapping on the box, "Oh God! That Chick's so cheap!"

"What?"

Meg gestured to the box. "This plastic has poinsettias on it."

Babe looked at the red and green poinsettias on the plastic and growled with disgust. Chick was known all through Hazlehurst for her tightness. She was forever giving people gifts that she claimed "must've got broken when you opened it," and, of course, sending Peekay and Buck Jr. off to birthday parties with headless dolls and already-colored coloring books for presents.

Meg shook her head. "Poor Lenny. She needs some love in her life. All she does is work out at that brickyard and take care of Old Grandaddy."

Babe nodded as Meg slashed the plastic wrapping off the candy box. It seemed to Babe as though Lenny's relationship with Old Grandaddy had gotten progressively more peculiar since Meg had moved away from home, but she wasn't sure she wanted to tell Meg about it. How sometimes Lenny opened up a cot and slept in the upstairs hallway outside Old Grandaddy's room so she could hear him in the night if he took sick. But if Meg knew about that, she might start yelling at Lenny. Meg was always yelling at Lenny about being too nice to Old Grandaddy. And anyhow, Babe thought, Meg's already got enough to worry about what with me being a criminal. She doesn't need to know how easily Lenny is slipping into Old Grandmama's role. So all Babe said was, "Lenny's so shy with men."

Meg snorted. "Probably because of that *shrunken* ovary she has."

Babe smiled in spite of herself. "Yeah, that *deformed* ovary."

Staring out toward the garden at Lenny, Meg remembered the day Lenny had first found out from a doctor about her ovary problem. She had been around seventeen and hadn't seemed to care too much about it one way or the other. But then Old Grandaddy had told her how important it was to men that women have two working ovaries, and how probably Lenny should rule out any plans for marriage since no man would ever want to marry her. "But I will always give you a home, child," he had told Lenny.

Not sure whether Babe knew who had started all of Lenny's paranoias about her ovary, Meg said, "Old Grandaddy's the one who made her feel self-conscious about it. It's his fault. The old fool."

Babe didn't reply. She knew that Old Grandaddy wanted Lenny at home to take care of him, to be Old Grandmama for him, but what was there to be done about it? Babe really didn't want to encourage Meg to start on Lenny. Babe's role in the family had always been that of the go-between, smoothing things over with Lenny and Meg when Meg would shout at Lenny about being weak and spineless.

Babe glanced at Meg. Meg had opened Lenny's box of cremes and was casually nibbling away at the chocolates. Meg, noticing Babe's gaze directed toward the chocolates, extended the box with a smile. "Candy?"

"No thanks," Babe said.

Meg shrugged, bit into another creme, then

sighed. "God," she said. "You know what? I bet Lenny's never even slept with a man. Bet she's never even had it once."

Babe giggled slyly. "Oh, I don't know," she taunted. "Maybe she's had it once."

Meg sat up very straight. "She has?"

"Maybe. I think so."

"When? *When?*"

But Babe looked away coyly. "Well . . . maybe I shouldn't say."

"Babe!"

For a fraction of a second, Babe struggled with her conscience. Should she or should she not keep the secret she had sworn never to tell? On the one hand, Lenny had sworn her to never tell *anyone*. On the other hand, Meg truly wasn't just *anyone* . . .

Babe spun to Meg with eagerness. "All right then!" And, very rapidly, "It was after Old Grandaddy went back to the hospital this second time. Lenny calls me up to come over and to bring my Polaroid camera."

Babe recalled the day for Meg with relish—how Babe had hurried over to the house with her camera only to find Lenny in the sun parlor all dressed up in her very best Sunday clothes, her hair set, her nails polished, her eyelashes dabbed with mascara. She was sitting in a chair with a tea service laid out beautifully before her on a table. There was also a plate of homemade nut cookies which Lenny was chewing away at nervously upon Babe's arrival.

At first Babe had thought maybe Lenny was planning on entertaining some friends of Old Grandaddy's from the Methodist church and wanted the camera so she could take some snapshots of the friends to give to Old Grandaddy at the hospital. But no. After much hemming and hawing, Lenny had come clean. Swearing Babe never to tell a soul, she had explained that she wanted Babe to take a picture of her sitting behind the tea service so that she could mail the photo to Lonely Hearts of the South, a club Lenny had seen advertised in a magazine.

Meg listened to Babe's story with rapt attention as she continued to eat bits of Lenny's birthday candy.

"So," Babe was saying, "two weeks later she receives in the mail this whole load of pictures of available men, most of 'em fairly odd looking . . ."

Lenny and Babe had lined all the pictures up on Lenny's bed with eagerness in search of someone tall, dark, and handsome. Unfortunately, what the pictures had revealed were men with every possible human deformity—some with double sets of teeth, others with strange, swollen sores on their bald, ancient skulls. Both Lenny and Babe had been very disappointed in the pickings, and in the end Lenny had decided to give up on Lonely Hearts of the South and had thrown all the photographs of the peculiar men into the trash.

"But one of 'em," Babe explained to Meg, "this Charlie Hill from Memphis, Tennessee, well, he calls her up."

Meg, eating away with abandon now at the candy, smiled expectantly. "He does?"

Babe grinned and nodded. "Well, he drives down here to Hazlehurst 'bout three or four different times and has supper with her. Then one weekend"—and here Babe's voice dropped low and became urgent—"she goes up to Memphis to visit him and I think that is where *it* happened."

"What makes you think so?"

Babe leaned close to Meg and whispered, "Well, when I went to pick her up at the bus depot, she ran off the bus and threw her arms around me and started crying and sobbing as though she'd never like to stop. I asked her, I said, 'Lenny, what's the matter?' And she said, 'I have done it!' "

"And you think she meant that she'd done *it*?"

Babe nodded happily. "I think so."

Meg turned and looked out the window at Lenny, who was still on her knees in the garden. "Well, goddamn," she murmured. And then both Meg and Babe began to laugh with glee at the thought of their older sister finally bursting forth from her spinsterly cocoon and having a wild, lustful weekend in Memphis with a man named Charlie.

Finally, controlling her laughter, Babe continued. "But she didn't say anything else about it. She just went on to tell me about the boot factory where Charlie worked and what a nice city Memphis was."

"So what happened to this Charlie?"

In a flash Babe's eyes turned angry and her voice became sad. "Well, he came to Hazlehurst just one more time. Lenny took him over to meet Old Grandaddy at the hospital and after that they broke it off."

" 'Cause of Old Grandaddy?"

Babe shrugged. "Well, *she* said it was on account of her missing ovary. That Charlie didn't want to marry her on account of it."

Meg closed her eyes. Leave it to Old Grandaddy to start in on the ovary talk. The man would do anything to keep Lenny at home with him. But why did this Charlie have to go and fall for Old Grandaddy's talk and drop Lenny? "How mean," Meg said. "How *hateful*."

"Oh it was," Babe agreed, remembering how Lenny had cried and cried for days after she and Charlie had broken off. "He seemed like such a nice man, too . . . kinda chubby, with red hair and freckles, always telling these funny jokes."

"Hmmm," Meg said, more to herself than to Babe. "That doesn't seem right. Something about that doesn't seem exactly right."

Babe looked at Meg questioningly, but Meg only shrugged. It wasn't that she knew what wasn't exactly right about the story, it was just a feeling she had about sweet, pudgy men like Charlie and shy, slope-shouldered women like Lenny. Somehow, it seemed to Meg that people like that, people who had waited so many years to find someone who would love them and touch them and laugh with them, didn't let go of each other as easily as Charlie had let go of Lenny. There had to be something more, something Old Grandaddy had done that went beyond talking about the ovary problem. Or something Lenny herself had said . . .

Babe and Meg sat quietly looking out at Lenny in the garden, their thoughts full of their sister and her problems. Neither of them even heard a car pulling up to the house and stopping. Which was just as well, because the car contained a young man who was about to remind them that Lenny's difficulties in finding a man were really the least of the Magrath sisters' troubles.

Barnette Lloyd didn't know the meaning of the word *casual*. To every action in his life, the twenty-six-year-old lawyer brought a kind of single-minded intensity that tended—as often as not—to terrify people. To watch Barnette walking to the public library was to see a man possessed by a thirst for knowledge; to observe him brushing his teeth was to understand the depth with which an individual could commit himself to proper oral hygiene; and to go grocery shopping with him was to realize that the selection of a breakfast cereal could actually be one of life's gravest tasks.

There was a rumor in Hazlehurst—a false one actually—that as a child Barnette had worn a three-piece suit on a hayride and had admonished the other children for not taking the ride seriously enough. But if that rumor was idle, others weren't: Barnette *did* have the highest I.Q. in all of Copiah County; he *was* inclined to forget to blink; and he *had* had a crush on Babe Botrelle ever since he had first seen her at a Christmas church bazaar.

So it was that as Barnette got out of his car and began walking to the Magrath house to talk with Babe about what happened to be his first real law case, he was not only typically fanatical in the way he marched along the sidewalk, he was even *atypically* fanatical. He gripped his briefcase like a man clutching a million-dollar gem, stared ahead of him at the house's front door as though he intended to burn it down with his eyes, and finally pounded up the steps with a sense of urgency and mission seldom seen even in the most dedicated of combat soldiers.

"Hello, hello!" he called out with the deepest voice he could muster. "Is anybody home?"

Babe and Meg, still sitting on the back porch watching Lenny garden, glanced up. Babe turned to Meg with a look that held deep fright. "Who's that?" she whispered.

Meg started to say she didn't have the foggiest notion who it could be, but before she had even opened her mouth, Babe was running to the front of the house.

"Hello!" shouted Barnette, craning his neck toward a window in an effort to see inside the house. "Hello! Mrs. Botrelle?"

Babe stopped in the middle of the living room the moment she caught a glimpse of Barnette's piercing eyes. Twice already she had seen those eyes. Both times she had been standing in her prison cell and had succeeded in evading their glare only by running over to her tiny cot and hurling her blanket over her head.

Meg caught up with Babe and put her arm around her little sister's back.

"Shoot," Babe whispered. "It's that lawyer. I don't want to see him."

Meg looked at Babe questioningly. "Oh Babe, come on," she whispered back. "You've got to see him sometime."

"No I don't," replied Babe, and in a flash she was running away from Meg, heading toward the bedroom stairs. Meg started to chase after her, but Babe was faster, and tore up the steps like a hunted rabbit, stopping only when she had reached the landing to yell down, "Tell him I died!"

"Oh Babe!" Meg called in frustration up the stairs. "Will you come back here? *Babe!*"

Meg heard the bedroom door bang shut.

"Ah shit," she muttered. And just what was she supposed to do now? Drag Babe down the steps by her hair? Tie her in a chair and force her to talk about Zackery?

Barnette was still knocking. "Mrs. Botrelle?"

For a moment Meg stood helpless and furious, then she balled up her fists and walked quickly to the door. Not in the least knowing what she would say, she swung the door open and stepped onto the front porch, only to be shocked when she ran almost smack into someone who resembled nothing so much as a teenage mortician.

Surely, Meg thought, taking in Barnette's dark suit and grim, youthful face, this odd-looking child can't be my sister's attorney. "Hey . . . ah, hi," Meg said.

Barnette extended his right hand to Meg as though it were a knight's rapier. "How do you do," he said as Meg leaped back from the thrust of his hand. "I'm Barnette Lloyd."

Holy Christ, Meg thought, reluctantly forcing herself to move forward and accept Barnette's overly firm palm. Babe's probably going to wind up in the electric chair if this weirdo defends her.

But to Barnette she said, "Pleased to meet you. I'm Meg Magrath, Babe's older sister."

"Yes, I know," said Barnette, staring gravely into Meg's eyes. "You're the singer."

Meg nodded. "Well . . . yes," she said, as unnerved by his knowledge as by his unblinking gaze.

Barnette inclined his head toward her. "I came to hear you five different times when you were singing at that club in Biloxi. Greeny's, I believe, was the name of it."

"Yes," Meg said, a little overwhelmed, "Greeny's."

"There was something so sad and moving about how you sang those songs," Barnette said passionately, his eyes positively bulging. "It was like you had some special sort of vision."

"Why . . . thanks," Meg said, half wanting to take his words seriously, half wanting to lock him up in an institution. She cleared her throat. "Now. About Babe's case."

Barnette gripped his briefcase even tighter. "Yes?"

"Well," Meg said nervously. "We've just got to win it."

"I intend to," Barnette replied with absolute conviction.

Meg noticed that his knuckles were white from gripping his case. "Of course," she said. "But, ah . . . ah, you know you're *very* young."

"Yes I am. I'm young."

"It's just I'm concerned, Mr. Lloyd . . ."

Barnette took a step toward her. "Barnette," he said. "Please."

"Barnette," Meg said, backing away from him.

"Well, Barnette, it's, ah, just maybe we need someone with, well, with more experience. Someone totally familiar with the ins and outs and the this and the that of the legal dealings . . . And such as that."

Barnette narrowed his eyes. "You have reservations."

Meg smiled with relief. "Reservations! Yes! I have reservations!"

Barnette nodded sagely. "Well," he began with confidence, "possibly it would help you to know that I graduated first in my class from Ole Miss Law School. I also spent three different summers taking advanced courses in criminal law at Harvard Law School. I made *A*'s in all the given courses."

Meg glanced at Barnette. Sweat was breaking out on his neck and forehead and the veins at his temple were throbbing zealously. She could plainly see how desperately he wanted to take on Babe's case, and not wanting to break the heart of someone who had, after all, come to see her sing *five* times, she decided to give him a chance. "Relax," she told him. "Relax, Barnette." And sitting herself down in a wicker chair: "Let me think this out. Now, just how would you intend to get Babe off? You know, keep her out of jail."

Barnette walked quickly over to Meg. "It seems to me that we can get her off with a plea of self-defense, or possibly we could go with innocent by reason of temporary insanity."

Meg nodded and began rummaging for a cigarette. No sooner did she find one than Barnette was leaning over her with a match, his eyes glowing brighter than the lit stick in his hand. "But basically," he went on excitedly, "I intend to prove that Zackery Botrelle brutalized and tormented this poor woman to such an extent that she had no recourse but to defend herself in the only way she knew how."

"I like that," said Meg, inhaling on her cigarette with pleasure.

"Then of course," Barnette continued, "I'm hoping this will break the ice and we'll be able to go on to prove that the man's a total criminal as well as an abusive bully and a contemptible slob."

Meg, who had never been wild about Zackery, grinned and nodded. "That sounds good. To me that sounds very good."

Barnette almost smiled. "It's just our basic game plan," he said modestly.

For a moment, Meg leaned back in her wicker chair with happy visions of her piglike brother-in-law sitting behind bars. Quickly, though, reality caught up with her. You couldn't just go and make up stories about Zackery because it would make your life easier, could you? "But now," she said, "how are you going to prove all this about Babe being brutalized? We don't want anyone to commit perjury."

Barnette's eyes turned very dark. "Perjury? According to my sources, there'll be no need for perjury."

Meg stared at Barnette with confusion. "You mean . . . it's the truth?"

"This is a small town, Miss Magrath. The word gets out."

Meg's ears began to ring. "It's *really* the truth?"

Barnette opened his briefcase and removed a folder. "Just look at this. It's a photostatic copy of Mrs. Botrelle's medical chart over the past four years."

Meg grabbed the folder and stared with horror at page after page of broken bones, bruises, cuts, gashes, and slashes. "What . . ." she said hoarsely. "This is madness!" And to Barnette: "Did he do this to her?"

Barnette said nothing.

"I'll kill him!" Meg cried out. "I'll fry his blood! Did he do this?"

Alarmed by an intensity he had never seen in someone other than himself, Barnette took the folder away from Meg and tried to calm her. "To tell you the truth, I can't say for certain what was accidental and what was not. That's why I need to talk with Mrs. Botrelle. That's why it's *very* important that I see her."

Meg glanced at the front door, then back to Barnette. Well, she thought, he's definitely strange and possibly crazed, but he's got the goods on Zackery and he does seem to be passionate about the case and . . .

Yeah, Meg decided. Barnette was the lawyer for Babe, and she should talk to him. Only before that could happen, Meg knew she was going to have to have a talk with Babe first and find out what it was her sister was so desperately trying to hide.

Five

The graveyard was full of magnificent, carved headstones, but Babe didn't look at a single one of the glorified monuments. Instead she placed her hand-picked bouquet at a tiny marker that bore the words MARGARET DECKER MAGRATH, 1935–1967.

Babe had been eight when her mother died. It had hurt her that Mama had the puniest headstone in the cemetery. As though Mama hadn't been the most important person in the world—hadn't braided Babe's hair and kissed away her scrapes and done the little piggies with her toes. Mama should have had the biggest and best stone of all. Maybe a pink one with gold stars and silver lettering. Something nice and pretty like that. But since all she had was a sad gray slab, Babe had vowed she would make up for the drabness of the stone by keeping it bright with fresh flowers. So every week, rain or shine, Babe came to the graveyard with a bouquet.

Arranging the flowers, Babe smiled. It was nice to be here alone with Mama in the sunshine. Much better than over at Lenny's with Meg banging away on the bedroom door for

Babe to come out and talk. Babe had shoved blankets under the crack below the door to keep Meg's demanding questions away from her, but finally her voice just got to be too much and Babe had decided to shimmy down the pillar of the terrace and escape here to the graveyard.

Suddenly, a shadow loomed over Babe's head. Terrified, she looked up, only to see Meg—panting and angry—looking straight at her. "What did Zackery do to you?" Meg asked for what seemed to Babe to be the zillionth time that morning. "Did he hurt you?"

Babe sighed and returned to arranging her flowers. How had Meg found her? Meg never used to come to the graveyard when she lived at home. Babe was surprised Meg even knew where it was. She must have seen me running over here, she thought.

"Did he?" Meg was asking. And taking Babe's face and turning it toward her own: "Goddamnit, Babe . . ."

Babe looked down at the date of her mother's death. Then, worn out from all of Meg's questions and feeling too tired to keep running, she whispered, "Yes, he did."

Tears shot into Meg's eyes. *"Why?"* Then more gently, "Why?"

Babe shrugged. "I just started finding it impossible to laugh at his jokes the way I used to. I'd fall asleep just listening to him at the dinner table. He'd say, 'Hand me some of that gravy!' Or, 'This roast beef is too damn bloody.' And suddenly I'd be out cold like a light."

Meg stared at Babe for a moment. Had one of Zackery's blows done something to Babe's mind?

What did this nonsense about roast beef have to do with anything? "Oh Babe. Babe, this is very important. I want you to tell me what all happened right before you shot Zackery."

Babe made a face. "I told you I can't tell you on account of I'm protecting someone."

"But Babe! You've just got to talk to someone about all this. You just do."

"Why?" Babe asked innocently.

"Because it's a human need," Meg explained. "To talk about our lives. It's an important human need."

Babe considered this information for a time. There did seem to be some truth to what Meg was saying. Finally, a little reluctantly, she nodded. "All right. Well, do you remember Willie Jay?"

Meg didn't.

"Cora's youngest boy?" Babe added.

Vaguely, Meg could recall a tiny black child who had occasionally come along with his mother to the Magrath house when Cora had ironed for Old Grandmama. "Oh yeah. That little kid we used to pay a nickel to, to run down to the drugstore and bring us back a cherry Coke."

Babe smiled. "Right. Well, Cora irons at my place on Wednesdays now, and she just happened to mention that Willie Jay'd picked up this old stray dog and that he'd gotten real fond of him. But now they couldn't afford to feed him anymore, so she was gonna have to tell Willie Jay to set him loose in the woods."

"Uh-huh," Meg said, hoping that somehow, some way, this story might turn out to have more of a point than the one about the roast beef.

"Well, I said I liked dogs, and if he wanted to bring the dog over here, I'd take care of him."

"Uh-huh," Meg said again, tapping her fingers impatiently against a headstone.

"So the next day Willie Jay brings over this skinny, old dog with these little crossed eyes." And here Babe crossed her own eyes and did her best to show the dog's pathetic physique. "Well, I asked Willie Jay what his name was, and he said they called him Dog."

Meg drummed the gravestone harder. "Uh-huh."

"Yeah. Anyway, when Willie Jay was leaving, he gave Dog a hug and said, 'Good-bye, Dog. You're a fine old dog.' Well, I just felt something for him, so I told Willie Jay he could come back and visit with Dog anytime he wanted and his face just kinda lit right up. Anyhow, time goes on and Willie Jay keeps coming over and over. And we talk about Dog and how fat he's getting and then, well, you know, things start up."

Instantly, Meg's fingers stopped drumming. "No," she said numbly. "I don't know. What things start up?"

Babe turned pink. With a smile she whispered, "Well, things start up. Like sex. Like that."

Meg swallowed hard and stared at Babe incredulously, but Babe only continued to smile and blush. She's gone mad, Meg thought, attempting to picture Babe rolling about in the canopy bed at Botrelle mansion with a second-grader. "Babe, wait a minute. Willie Jay's a *boy*. A *small* boy." And holding her hand to her own waist: "About *this* tall."

But Babe only giggled. "No! Oh, no! He's taller now! He's fifteen now. When you knew him, he was only about seven or eight."

But Babe's explanation didn't totally appease Meg. "Even so . . . fifteen! And he's a black boy; a colored boy; a *Negro*."

"Well, I realize that, Meg," Babe said, a little flustered to think that Meg would believe she was so dumb as to have to be told what color Willie Jay was. "Why do you think I'm so worried about his getting public exposure? I don't want to ruin his reputation."

Meg looked at Babe's childlike face with a mixture of shock and disbelief. "I'm amazed. I'm really completely amazed. I didn't even know you were a liberal."

Now it was Babe's turn to be shocked: "Well, I'm not! I'm not a liberal! I'm a democratic!"

A democratic? Meg thought. Yes indeedy. One of those blows from Zackery has shaken the screws loose from Babe's head.

Babe was staring at some of the more elaborate headstones in the cemetery—gargoyles perched atop granite crosses, fat angels attached like bookends to enormous marble slabs. She felt extremely sad. Meg didn't seem to understand about Willy Jay, or even about Dog for that matter. Closing her eyes, Babe pictured herself walking along through the Botrelle mansion day after day, and she slowly related her tale to Meg. The first few months after her wedding hadn't been so bad. She would take tours of the different rooms and there had been a maid about her own age she had talked to often. Then Zackery had decided it was improper for Babe to do what he called "fraternizing with the help," and he had fired the maid. So Babe took her tours alone and didn't talk to anyone. Up and down the long corridors she went, trying to amuse herself by staring at formal portraits of Zackery's fat ancestors until the eyes in the portraits seemed to blink. Sometimes, Zackery's sister Lucille would show up and mistake Babe's stares for an interest in the Botrelle family's history. Then Babe would have to sit for hours as Lucille droned on about her great-grandaunt Agatha who had managed to keep the plantation running efficiently during the Civil War by feeding her two hundred slaves the leftover water from the vats in which she boiled potatoes for herself. "Potato water is actually all Negroes need to eat," Lucille would say. "Oh, they enjoy a little watermelon and fried chicken, but actually their constitutions are such that they can live for *centuries* on potato water."

Babe sighed and turned to Meg. "I was just lonely," she said. And then, picturing Willie Jay quite vividly: "And he was *so* good. I'd never had it that good. We'd always go into the garage and—"

"It's okay," Meg broke in, more than a little blown away by the look of extreme pleasure she could see entering Babe's eyes. "I've got the picture; I have *got* the picture. Now, let's just get back to the story. To when you shot Zackery."

Babe nodded pleasantly. "All right then. Let's see . . ." And narrowing her eyes, she tried to remember. "Willie Jay was over. And it was after we'd—"

"Yeah," Meg said quickly. "Yeah."

"Well, we were just standing around on the back porch playing with Dog . . ."

As Babe spoke, everything began to come back to her—the warmth of the day; the lazy, calm feeling inside her; the wiry, taut muscles in Willie Jay's shoulders. She could picture Willie Jay as he had stood beside her on the back veranda of the Botrelle mansion, his big eyes full of warmth. He'd been telling her his dreams for the future, how he wanted to go to college and become a professor of veterinary medicine or go to Nashville and become a country-western star. He'd been discussing the pros and cons of his career choices—how it would be nice to come up with vaccines for chickens and whatnot, but how it would perhaps be even nicer to appear on the stage of the Grand Ole Opry in a flame-red cowboy hat and have millions of women banging on his stage door, throwing him diamonds and telephone numbers and all that other star stuff. His mother was trying to urge him toward veterinary school. Babe had thought he could and should do both things—go to school by day and be a star at night—and Willie Jay had smiled broadly at her, his career problems solved, and had taken a jelly bean from his pocket and tossed it high into the air with pleasure. Babe had been impressed by the way he'd caught the bean in his mouth and asked for her own jelly bean. But when she'd tried Willy Jay's trick, her jelly bean had skittered off the veranda, rolled onto the lawn where Dog had rushed after it avariciously. With big, sagging jowls, Dog had chewed the jelly bean. Babe and Willie Jay had laughed, and were soon tossing all kinds of jelly beans Dog's way.

Suddenly, Babe had felt a chill and had shivered. About to ask Willie Jay if he, too, was feeling a fast change in the weather, she had spun around, only to see a tremendous, dark shadow approaching her.

It was Zackery and his huge, jiggly stomach.

Narrowing his small, beady eyes at Willie Jay, he had said, "Hey boy, what are you doing here?"

Terrified, Willie Jay had looked down at the ground.

Babe could see beads of sweat forming over Zackery's lips. She knew those sweat drops, knew they came when Zackery was feeling his cruelest. "He's not doing anything!" she had shouted. And to Willie Jay: "You just go home, Willie Jay. You just run right on home."

But Willie Jay had lingered just a moment too long, maybe seeing the fear in Babe's eyes, maybe just feeling fear himself. In any event, in a flash Zackery was slamming Babe aside and lurching toward Willie Jay.

Holding his big, black briefcase like a weapon in his hands, Zackery stood over Willie Jay. Blam! The briefcase cracked at Willie Jay's face, sending the boy reeling down the steps of the veranda.

Dog, his mouth still stuffed with the jelly

beans, tried to yelp, but his little cries came out muted.

Willie Jay had skidded across the concrete. His elbows ripped open. He'd looked from his bleeding arms to Zackery, and his soft brown eyes had filled with tears of rage.

Zackery had smiled icily at Willy Jay's tears. Babe had seen that smile hundreds of times when she herself had been crying after one of his blows, and it had always scared her, made her freeze with submission. But seeing that smile aimed at Willie Jay didn't make her scared; it made her sick and mad. With all her energy, she had leaped at Zackery, but he had somehow anticipated the leap and tossed her aside as though she weighed no more than a toy doll. She had stumbled onto Dog, who had managed to finish eating the jelly beans and had started yelping in pain.

Zackery kicked out at Willie Jay viciously, dug his boots into the boy's teary face as hard and mean and rapidly as he could. Willie Jay kept trying to get up off the ground, but Zackery's kicks would send him smashing back onto the concrete over and over. At last, Willie Jay lay writhing in pain and humiliation, and accepted the blows, while Zackery spoke in a low growl: "Don't you ever come around here again, or I'll have them cut out your gizzard."

Babe had been lying half atop Dog, half across the base of a pillar. Her body ached. She kept trying to pull herself up, but she couldn't.

At last, Willie Jay had begun to crawl away. For a few moments, Zackery pursued him, but then Willie Jay was on his feet running, and Zackery's heavy, heaving body came to a halt.

Babe had finally managed to stand up. The last she had seen of Willie Jay, he had been running across the yard in agony. Dog had been following, barking loudly.

Now, standing in the cemetery with Meg, Babe's eyes filled with tears. She began walking quickly away, stumbling along the headstones, but Meg pursued her. At last, Babe stopped walking and said, "After that, I don't remember much too clearly. Let's see . . ."

Babe closed her eyes. What had happened after Willie Jay had left? Zackery had walked off somewhere. To the kitchen? Someplace. Babe had continued standing on the veranda, swollen and aching. Then, not even knowing why, she had found herself going into the house, heading for the dining room.

She explained to Meg how she had felt as though she were moving underwater, swimming slowly through the dining room. Everything about the room had looked vivid and strange to her—the glittering chandelier trembling as Zackery pounded around in another part of the house; the brocade curtains blowing at the window; the dark oak paneling of the room shining out, giving Babe her own reflection as she headed steadily toward a small desk at the farthest end of the room.

Inside a drawer of the desk, Babe had found a pistol. She had stared at the gun a moment, not quite knowing why she was even looking at it, then had taken it into her hand, cocked it, and held it to her own ear like a deadly seashell.

Meg stared at Babe with wide eyes. But Babe kept talking, now with mounting excitement: "Why, I was gonna shoot off my own head! *That's* what I was gonna do! Then I heard the back door slamming and suddenly, for some reason, I thought about Mama . . . how she'd hung herself. And here I was about ready to shoot myself. Then I realized . . . that's right, I realized how I didn't *want* to kill myself."

Babe spun toward her mother's drab headstone and looked at it with amazement. "And Mama," she whispered, "she probably didn't want to kill *her*self. She wanted to kill *him*, and I wanted to kill him, too. I wanted to kill Zackery, not myself. 'Cause I . . . I wanted to live!"

Meg's heart pounded as she listened to Babe tell how she had taken the gun down from her ear and used it to gently brush away some curls that had slid onto her damp forehead. Then Babe had held the gun straight out from her chest and waited for Zackery to come into the living room. As she had stood there, she hadn't felt any fear whatsoever. In fact, she had felt peaceful for the first time since her wedding night. And she'd thought back over the years since that wedding night—how Zackery had used her as a human punching bag every time something hadn't worked out for him either on the job or even on the golf course; how she had tried to cover all her bruises with makeup and the prettiest and pinkest clothes she could find; how hard she had tried to keep smiling in front of Lenny and Old Grandaddy. And how good it felt to know she wasn't going to have to hide or fake smiles ever again.

At last the dining-room door had swung open.

Zackery had grinned when he saw the gun in Babe's hand, and kept grinning as she walked steadily toward him, her finger on the trigger. Then, when Babe had gotten halfway to him, he had shaken his head with condescension and said, "You little idiot."

And that had been all it had taken. Just those three little words—three little words Babe had been hearing for six years but now had no intention of ever hearing again.

She pulled her finger as hard as she could on the trigger and the gun exploded with sound as Zackery crashed against a shelf full of china and then against a drop-leaf table.

Seeing that he was still alive, Babe had pulled the trigger again, but all the gun did that time was click.

Zackery crouched on his knees, clutching at his side. Sweat dripped from his face as he lifted his hand from his side to examine the wound. The hand was covered with blood.

Whether it was actual pain from the bullet hole or just the sight of his own blood on his hand that made Zackery faint, Babe wasn't sure, but faint he did.

Now, Babe glanced at Meg with a look that asked, "You want to hear more?" And Meg, her eyes both terrified and relieved, nodded weakly.

Barnette was proud of his tiny law office, but not quite so proud of it that the thought of Babe Botrelle actually entering it didn't fill him with terror. In Barnette's mind, only heaven was a suitable place for Babe's small, pink-shoed feet. And so, when he received a call from Meg saying that Babe had at last agreed to talk with him and would be at his office sometime in the late afternoon, he had gone on a manic spree of cleaning and organizing.

With Windex and Mr. Clean in hand, he had earnestly scrubbed every bit of floor and wall and ceiling. Then, just to be on the safe side, he had fled to the store for a spray can of room deodorizer, with which he proceeded to douse not only the room, but also his own body. Next he set about organizing his few, meager possessions. He put his law books out on a giant-sized shelf that made them look puny and ridiculous to his eyes; he adjusted his college and law school degrees on the wall so that they hung exactly even; and he arranged his rather badly scratched-up desk with a fresh, inviting pile of business cards, a stack of crisply sharpened pencils, and a carefully scrubbed ashtray.

The furniture in the room had been bought used for Barnette by his mother, who had also seen fit to donate a large photograph of herself in order to make the office more attractive. The only other item of decoration was a Christmas angel made of delicate paper which Barnette kept off to one side of his office where he could sneak glances at it as he cleaned away.

At last, the office as close to perfect as Barnette could make it—which was actually *quite* close to perfect—he sat down behind his desk and awaited Babe's arrival. It seemed an eternity that he had to sit and listen for the *tap, tap, tap* of her tiny heels, but as soon as he rushed to the door and actually saw her wondrous, freckled face, he felt as though she shouldn't have come so soon, that he needed more time—eons more time—to prepare for someone as magnificent as the woman who stood before him. My God, he'd thought, you have brought Aphrodite to me.

Babe had smiled at him briefly, then asked for a Coke. Barnette had stared at her, horrified. A Coke? How could he have been such a mindless numbskull not to have bought her a dozen-nay, a hundred—Cokes! And without introducing himself or even so much as saying hello, he had raced from the office in search of a cola machine.

When he had returned, breathless and sweating, with a Coke *and* some Planter's Peanuts, Babe was sitting near his desk applying a fresh coat of pink lipstick to her perfect rosebud lips. He had watched her in awe for a time, then wordlessly thrust the Coke and nuts in her face. With a gloved hand, Babe had reached for the Coke, and even made an adorable squeaking sound in her throat when she saw the nuts.

Finally Barnette had introduced himself and the two had gotten down to business. Babe told him everything she had said to Meg earlier in the day, and he had listened to each word with devotion and had written down what she said with explosive intensity.

Not that it hadn't been hard for Barnette to concentrate. Every time he would glance up from his writing and see her pop another Planter's Peanut in her mouth, he had had to steel himself for the task at hand rather than lose himself in a daydream in which he was Willie Jay.

Now, the story of the shooting finished, Barnette gave in for just one brief moment to his fantasies, then turned beet red and hoarsely said, "Let's see, ah, where were we?"

Smiling daintily, Babe noticed his blush, turned a little pink herself, then coyly replied, "I just shot Zackery."

"Right. Correct," Barnette said, trying desperately to ignore the bangings of his heart. "You've just pulled the trigger."

Babe leaned back in her chair and crossed her legs demurely. "Tell me," she asked, "do you think Willie Jay can stay out of all this?"

Barnette nodded vigorously. "Believe me, it is in our interest to keep him as *far* out of this as possible.

"Good." Babe grinned.

Barnette started to grin back, then caught himself and sat up very straight. "All right," he said in his most authoritative voice, "you've just shot one Zackery Botrelle as a result of his continual physical and mental abuse . . . Now what happens?"

"Well, after I shot him," Babe said thoughtfully, "I put the gun down on the piano bench and then I went out into the kitchen and made up a pitcher of lemonade."

"Lemonade?"

Babe grinned again. "Yes." And confidentially: "I was just dying of thirst. My mouth was just as dry as a bone."

Barnette eyed Babe briefly, then cleared his

throat. "So in order to quench this *raging thirst* that was *choking you dry* and preventing *any possibility of you uttering intelligible sounds or phrases,* you went out to the kitchen and made up a pitcher of . . . lemonade."

"Right," Babe said sweetly, playing with a curl on her forehead. "I made it just the way I like it, with lots of sugar and lemon. Then I added two trays of ice and stirred it up with my wooden stirring spoon."

Barnette watched as Babe acted out each detail of lemonade preparation for him, from the slicing of the lemons to the stirring of the juice. And in spite of everything, he found himself mesmerized by the way her small gloved hands cracked pretend ice cubes from a pretend ice tray. "Then what?" he asked, trying to shake off her spell.

"Then I drank three glasses, one right after the other. They were large glasses, about this tall." And she demonstrated the size of each, lifting imaginary glass after glass and gulping at them as Barnette watched her Adam's apple slide up and down. "Then suddenly my stomach swoll all up. I guess what caused it was all that sour lemon."

Barnette stared as Babe rubbed her belly. "Could be," he whispered.

"Then what I did was I wiped my mouth off with the back of my hand, like this . . ." And she let her fingers slide across her rosebud lips.

Be still my heart, Barnette thought. Out loud he said—as professionally as he could—"Hmmmmm."

"I did it to clear off all those little beads of

water that had settled there," added Babe, mistaking Barnette's intent gaze at her lips as a sign of legal confusion.

"I see."

"Then I called out to Zackery . . ." And she proceeded to explain to Barnette how she had stood in the large kitchen, her empty glass in hand, and shouted, "Zackery! I've made some lemonade. Can you use a glass?"

Zackery had not responded. So, sighing, she had taken a clean glass from the cupboard, poured some lemonade into it, and brought it out to the dining room. There was Zackery, just where she had left him on the floor, still bleeding, only now he was conscious again. He had looked up at her, then begun a strange kind of moaning and grunting.

Babe had leaned over him. "What?" she had asked, unable to make out any words from the gurgling noises in his throat. "Lemonade?"

Zackery had shaken his head slowly.

"You don't want it?"

Zackery had shaken his head a bit more vigorously.

Well, Babe had thought, if he doesn't want this glass, maybe I'll just drink it. Still, she hadn't wanted to be rude, so she had leaned even closer to him, smiling a bit, and had asked, as politely as possible, "Would you like a Coke instead?"

Suddenly, Zackery's face had seem to explode with anger and he had begun making huge, furious gestures toward the telephone. For a moment, Babe watched his bulging, mean eyes and his violently flailing arm. She supposed he wanted her to call an ambulance for him. Still, it wasn't as though he had actually come right out and asked her. So she decided to drink just one more glass of lemonade . . . nice and slow.

Barnette wrote down everything Babe said, then looked up at her. She was staring out a small window in his office with a vaguely troubled expression on her face. "I guess that's gonna look kinda bad," she said quietly.

"What?" asked Barnette, curious as to just which of the countless self-incriminating factors of the case she was referring to.

"Me fixing that lemonade before I called the hospital."

"Well," Barnette began, hoping he wasn't lying to her, "not necessarily."

Babe knitted her brow in a manner that Barnette found hopelessly irresistible. "I'll tell you," she said, "I think the reason I made up the lemonade was 'cause I was afraid they would see that I had tried to shoot Zackery—in fact, that I *had* shot him, and they would accuse me of possible murder and send me away to jail."

Barnette nodded sympathetically. "Well, that's understandable."

"I think so." Then with a sense of wonderment: "I mean, in fact, that's just what *did* happen. Yes, here I am, just practically on the brink of utter doom. Why, I feel so alone."

Every inch of Barnette's body longed to leap across his desk, grab Babe in his arms, and embrace her fiercely and protectively. Instead he fumbled with a pencil, glanced uneasily at her, and said, "Now, now, look— Why there's no reason for you to get yourself all upset and worried."

Babe began to cry.

"Please don't," Barnette said softly. "Please."

Babe turned toward him. Something in the gentleness of his voice reminded her of Willie Jay. But those eyes! So strange, deep, and knowing—they scared Babe.

"Don't you worry, Mrs. Botrelle," Barnette said kindly. "We're going to have a solid defense."

Babe wiped away her tears and smiled shyly. "Please don't call me Mrs. Botrelle. My name's Becky. People in the family call me Babe; but my real name's Becky."

A slow smile formed on Barnette's face. Babe noticed the smile and returned it, thinking, Why his eyes aren't so scary at all when he takes to smiling. They're even real nice eyes, puppydog like.

Barnette could feel his underarms breaking into a sweat. Becky, he thought. Ah, Becky, Becky, if only I had sprayed human deodorizer on myself instead of room deodorizer, perhaps I could find the courage to touch you.

"Are you sure you didn't go to Hazlehurst High?" Babe asked, still gazing into Barnette's eyes.

"No, I went away to a boarding school."

"Gosh, you sure look familiar. You sure do."

Barnette turned toward the Christmas angel. "Well, I . . . I doubt you'll remember, but I did meet you once."

"You did? When?"

"At the Christmas bazaar, year before last. You were selling cakes and cookies and candy."

Babe clapped her hands together. "Oh yes! You bought the orange pound cake!"

"Right!"

"Of course, and then we talked for a while." And Babe smiled again as she remembered how Barnette had stuttered so sweetly when he'd spoken to her. "We talked about the Christmas angel."

"You do remember!" Barnette cried out passionately.

"I remember it very well," Babe replied with equal passion.

Suddenly the phone rang. Barnette glared at it a moment as though he wished to toss it from his window, but then caught control of himself and answered in his most professional tone. "Hello, this is Mr. Barnette Lloyd speaking."

"Yeah, well this is *Senator* Zackery Botrelle," said a low, slow voice. "You my wife's idiot lawyer?"

"Yes, that's correct," Barnette replied coolly. "I'm Mrs.—ah, *Becky's* attorney."

Babe gave Barnette an appreciative grin.

Zackery was saying, "Well, listen to this, Mr. Barnette Lloyd. You get your attorney butt over here around eight o'clock tonight and I'm gonna show you some real *blackening* evidence I've got against your little lily-white client."

Barnette tightened his jaw and turned his voice to steel. "Why certainly, Mr. Botrelle. I'd be more than glad to check out any pertinent information that you may have."

"Eight o'clock," Zackery growled, "or *Becky's* ass is grass."

"Fine. Good-bye."

Barnette hung up the phone and turned to Babe. She was staring out the window again, stricken with terror. Barnette wanted to go to her, to assure her that everything would be fine, but until night came and he was able to see the evidence Zackery had against her, he had no idea whether things would ever be fine for Babe again.

Six

Lenny was fit to be tied. All afternoon she had begged Meg to come on over with her to see Old Grandaddy at the hospital. Meg had rolled her eyes and offered a million excuses—everything from wanting to be home when Babe came back from her meeting with Barnette to being allergic to hospital rooms. At last Lenny had said fine, don't come, break Old Grandaddy's heart and see if I care. Lenny had started for the car alone with a box of cookies she had baked—without Meg's help of course—for the poor, suffering man. Then at the last minute Meg had run after the car, cigarette dangling from her mouth, denim jacket blowing free in the wind over her miniskirt, and had decided to come along.

"Not that I'm going to have anything to say to the mean old buzzard," Meg had said.

Lenny had replied that Meg shouldn't worry; Old Grandaddy probably wouldn't have anything to say to her either, especially after he'd gone and sent her all that money to come home for Christmas and hadn't even gotten a card in return for a thank-you.

Only that's not how things had worked out.

The moment Meg had walked into Old Grandaddy's room, she'd started chattering away a mile a minute. And not just any chatter either—lies. Lie after lie after lie spilled out of her mouth—how she had a house right next to that sign that spells out *Hollywood* up on a hill; how she had a heart-shaped swimming pool in back of the house which she liked to keep full of pink champagne; how the reason old Grandaddy hadn't noticed her when she was on Johnny Carson's show was on account of the fact that she had worn a wig and used an assumed name so her fans wouldn't mob her when she walked out on stage. And on and on until Lenny had wanted to scream.

But what bothered Lenny the most was the way Old Grandaddy had responded to all of this. All Meg had had to do was walk in the room and he was acting as though royalty had come for a visit. His eyes lit up; he tried to sit in his bed for the first time in weeks; and he even smiled—something Lenny herself had been unable to get him to do for years.

Now it was early evening. For more than two hours Lenny had been sitting in a corner of the hospital room, some kind of ghost or something as far as Meg and Old Grandaddy were concerned. Her back ached; her mouth was sore from trying to keep a strained smile on her face.

Meg was holding Old Grandaddy's hand as the two laughed and talked away about her "third hit record in a row."

"RCA's releasing the album this spring," Meg confided. "I'm gonna have my picture on the cover. I'm gonna be eating a big pineapple under a palm tree."

Old Grandaddy, sick and emaciated and watery-eyed but obviously having the time of his life, smiled proudly. "Now won't that be just cute as a bug," he said merrily. And then squeezing Meg's hand with all his strength: "Oh Lord, child, we sure have missed you. We thought you'd be here Christmas. I was mightily ashamed when you didn't come."

At last! Lenny thought. He finally confronts her about her selfish, selfish ways!

But Meg didn't so much as bat an eye, let alone wince. "Oh, I'm sorry, Old Grandaddy," she said offhandedly. "I really am. I tell you the reason I didn't use the money you sent me to come home Christmas was I was right in the middle of this huge multi-million-dollar motion picture. And I was just under too much pressure."

Lenny's jaw dropped. Motion picture indeed! And wasn't it only yesterday Meg had been saying she wasn't even working in show business anymore? I should interrupt right now, Lenny thought, and ask her whether she filmed the motion picture before or after she got off work from paying the cold storage bills at the dog food company.

But Old Grandaddy was talking. "Listen, don't you give Christmas another thought," he assured Meg. "Just tell me all about this new motion picture you're in."

Lenny rolled her eyes as Meg began her zillionth lie of the day. "Well . . . it's coming out in the spring and it's called *Singing in a Shoe Factory*. But I really don't have a large leading role," she explained modestly. "It's more of a small leading role."

Yes, Lenny thought, so small we might even call it nonexistent.

Meg continued to drone on. Lenny couldn't even bear to listen anymore, but instead stared at Old Grandaddy's happy eyes and wondered why it was people like Meg always came out on top while people like herself always came out on bottom.

The cookies Lenny had brought lay untouched on Old Grandaddy's bedstand. Lenny glanced at them. Poor little cookies, she thought. Nobody wants them. Nobody'll ever want them.

The sun was setting. Babe sat out on the screened-in porch of the Magrath house painting her nails the same shade of pink as the evening sky. She was smiling as she remembered saying good-bye to Barnette at his law office that afternoon.

He had stood nervously beside her at the door, his back ramrod straight, his manner extremely professional. Babe had thought maybe she'd been mistaken to have thought he liked her more than the average lawyer likes his average would-be-murderer type of client. But then when he had spoken his farewells, his voice had trembled, and she had known he was feeling something.

"Good-bye, Becky," Babe now said out loud, trying to recapture Barnette's exact intonations of romance and longing.

"Good-bye, Barnette," she whispered back to herself, trying to recapture her own intonations so she could know how her voice had sounded to his ears.

"Oooooh," she sighed. It had all been *so* beautiful.

Suddenly, the back door banged open. Babe could hear Lenny's footsteps moving toward her. "Lenny, hi!" she called out. "How's Old Grandaddy?"

"Oh, he's fine!" Lenny shouted back in a tone that was just a shade beyond fury. "He's wonderful! Never been better!"

Babe grimaced. Obviously something had happened between Meg and Lenny. She knew this partly because something always did.

In a moment, Lenny was out on the porch clutching the box of candy Chick had given her. Her face was almost white. She rattled the half-empty box at Babe with rage. "Who ate this candy?"

Babe looked down at the floor. "Meg," she whispered.

Lenny nodded and opened the box. "My *one* birthday present, and look what she does!" Then, peering at the candy indignantly: "Why, she's taken one little bite out of each piece and then just put it back in! Oooh! That's just like her!"

Babe glanced at the candy. It did look awfully pitiful. "Lenny, please . . ."

But Lenny couldn't contain herself. "I can't help it!" she cried, storming about the porch with the candy box. "It gets me mad! It gets me upset! Why, Meg has always run wild. She started smoking and drinking when she was fourteen years old. She never made good grades—never made her own *bed*!"

Babe continued painting her nails. She had heard this litany of complaints against Meg for years and knew that in a moment Lenny would be bringing up what everyone in the family referred to as "the jingle bell issue."

"But somehow," Lenny was saying, "Meg always seemed to get what she wanted. She's the one who always got singing and dancing lessons." And then, turning to Babe as though she were making a fresh discovery: "Why, do you remember how Meg always got to wear twelve jingle bells on her petticoats while we were only allowed to wear three apiece? *Why?*"

Babe shrugged and began to blow on her nails to dry them.

"Why should Old Grandmama let her sew twelve golden jingle bells on her petticoats and us only three?" Lenny asked.

"I don't know," Babe said, just as she had said countless times before to the same question. "Maybe she didn't jingle them as much."

Lenny shook her head. "I can't help it. It gets me mad."

So Babe tried another tack: "Things have been hard for Meg. After all, she was the one who found Mama."

But Lenny, who almost always could be calmed down about something Meg had done by being reminded of the horrible sight Meg had been forced to endure down in the cellar, remained livid. "Oh I know; she's the one who found Mama. But that's always been the excuse."

Babe eyed Lenny and sadly said, "But I tell you, Lenny, after it happened, Meg started doing all sorts of these strange things."

"Like what?"

Babe looked down at her nails and whispered, "Like things I never wanted to tell you about."

Lenny, forgetting her anger for a moment, stared at Babe with a curious, nervous look. What did Babe know about Meg that Lenny herself didn't know? "What sort of things?" she asked.

Babe leaned toward Lenny and hesitantly began to explain some of the peculiar things she had secretly observed Meg doing back in grade school. "Well, for instance, when we used to go over to the library, Meg would force herself to look through this old, black book called *Diseases of the Skin*. It was full of the most sickening pictures. Things like rotting-away noses and eyeballs drooping off down the sides of people's faces and scabs and sores and eaten-away places over *all* parts of people's bodies."

Lenny recoiled in horror. "Babe, please! That's enough!"

But Babe wouldn't stop. Maybe if Lenny understood some of the strange rituals Meg had performed after their mother's death, she'd begin to understand Meg better and wouldn't fight so much with her. For after finding Mama in the cellar of their Vicksburg house, Meg had deliberately begun to search for everything painful and ugly in life. She'd ride her bike to the slums over on the bad side of the tracks, would peer through hospital windows at dying cancer patients, would deliberately look at dead animals on the highway. Babe shook her head. "It was the same way she used to force herself to look at that poster of crippled children stuck up in the window at Dixieland Drugs."

Lenny looked perplexed.

"You know," Babe reminded her. "The one where they want you to give a dime. Meg would stand there and stare at their little crippled legs. Then she'd purposely go and spend her dime on a double-scoop ice cream cone and eat it all down. She'd say to me, 'See, I can stand it! I can stand it! Just look how I'm gonna be able to stand it!' "

Lenny looked at Babe blankly a moment. She could feel her anger toward Meg sliding away, moving toward something almost like understanding. Here, all these years, Lenny had been thinking Meg so hard, so tough, when all along her heart had been aching just like Lenny's. Why, Meg wasn't really so different from Lenny at all; she just had given herself a poker face.

But no sooner did Lenny start on the road to compassion than she happened to notice her chewed-up, disgusting box of birthday candy and all her anger came back again. What did it matter if Meg truly had a heart down deep? If Meg, too, had been hurt by Mama's bizarre death? Did that mean Meg had license to do whatever she wanted in life? Eat people's birthday candy? Tell lies? And—worst of all—go out of her way to cripple Doc Porter? "Well," she finally said to Babe, "I suppose you'd have to be a pretty hard person to be able to do what she did to Doc Porter."

Babe shook her head with exasperation. Why did Lenny and everyone else in town have to hold Meg responsible for Doc's bad leg? "Oh shoot! It wasn't Meg's fault that roof fell in and crunched Doc's leg. It wasn't her fault."

"Well, it was Meg who refused to evacuate.

She wanted to stay because she thought a hurricane would be . . . oh, I don't know . . . a lot of fun." And Lenny shook her head furiously, remembering how Meg had called her from Biloxi the day of the big hurricane and had gone on and on about what a great time she was having getting drunk with Doc while everyone else fled to basements of schools and churches. It hadn't once occurred to Meg that maybe it wasn't safe to party your way through the worst storm in decades. Worse, it hadn't crossed Meg's mind how cruel it was of her to tell Lenny about what it was like to drink huge glasses of bourbon and march along a pounding ocean holding Doc's big, warm hand.

Lenny turned away from Babe and looked out the porch window at the last flickers of sunlight. Then quietly she said, "Everyone says she baited Doc into staying with her. She said she'd marry him if he'd stay."

Babe had never heard this, and she looked shaken. She had always believed that anything Meg did that hurt someone was an accident. It scared her to think maybe Meg could be deliberately so mean as to promise her love-struck boyfriend such a thing. "Well," she said at last, "he has a mind of his own. He could have gone."

Lenny turned quickly to Babe. "But he didn't!" she cried out. And then, with tears in her eyes, " 'Cause . . . 'cause he loved her."

Babe nodded hesitantly. So Lenny was still in love with Doc. Or at least still in love with the hope of being adored by someone as fiercely and passionately as Doc had adored Meg. And why shouldn't Lenny still dream of love? Babe thought. If I, a woman on the brink of life imprisonment, can still hope for a happy heart, why shouldn't poor Lenny?

Babe opened her mouth to say something about how maybe Lenny shouldn't hold it against Meg that Doc had loved Meg, but Lenny went on. "And then Meg left. She just left him there to leave for California. 'Cause of her career, she says. It took almost a year for Doc's leg to heal and after that he gave up his medical career altogether. He said he was tired of hospitals."

Babe nodded. She remembered how Lenny had gone to see Doc at the hospital, had baked him cookies, had written funny notes and things. But then Lenny had stopped visiting with him on account of all Doc had wanted to talk about when he had seen Lenny was whether she had heard from Meg or not. That was about when Lenny had begun to lavish all her attention on Old Grandaddy. But, of course, all Old Grandaddy liked to do, too, was talk about Meg and her wonderful adventures in Hollywood.

Gosh, Babe thought, I surely do hope Meg and Lenny manage to patch things up before I go to the gas chamber or the electric chair or wherever it is people like me go.

As for Lenny, she returned to staring out the porch window. She tried to turn her mind to things other than Meg, but all she could think was, just wait until that sister of mine puts her foot through the door . . .

Seven

Night had come to Hazlehurst; and so, finished with their suppers, the residents of the town had taken to their porches to discuss the evening paper's banner headline: SENATOR BOTRELLE IN STABLE CONDITION! WIFE OUT ON BAIL!

Most everybody in town was a little depressed to learn that Zackery apparently intended to live. Prospects for national coverage of the shooting were starting to look bleak. Of course, no one was willing to give up hope that this Magrath crime might prove as exciting and juicy as the one sixteen years back. Already a rumor was beginning to creep about that there was some kind of racial motive to the blasting of the hole in Zackery's stomach.

But what was truly keeping the population cheerful and full of gossip was the return of Meg Magrath, Hazlehurst's favorite bad-girl-come-home. Up and down the street where the Magraths lived, porches were full with folks who had received phone calls announcing that Meg had been spotted at the local liquor store and was walking home—*with a bottle of bourbon at her lips.* Breathless and expectant, the good people of Hazlehurst had hurried over to any friendly porch they could find to take in the sight of what they hoped would be a drunk and stumbling Meg headed for home.

Meg did not exactly disappoint her crowd. Though she wasn't actually drunk, she did lope along the sidewalk chugging at the bourbon, which she was keeping—none too discreetly—in a paper sack.

Meg noticed people staring at her, but their prying eyes meant nothing to her. She had long since stopped caring about rude looks and words. In her teens, it would sometimes make her flesh crawl when she'd hear somebody say, "That's the one that had to take Mary off the clothesline," or "You know she's the Magrath who saw *the cat*." But no more. Now all that got to Meg was what was waiting for her at home. She knew Lenny was going to have a fit when she walked in. And she was also troubled about Babe.

Bourbon hadn't been the only thing Meg had gotten at the store on her walk back from the hospital. Babe had asked her to pick up a copy of the newspaper. It bothered Meg the way Babe had seemed kind of—well, happy—to learn she was going to be the featured news story that night. Meg had told Babe that probably looking at the newspaper would just depress her, but Babe had been adamant about wanting to read about the shooting.

As Meg approached the Magrath house she saw a light shining in the sisters' bedroom. So that's where Lenny's waiting for me, she thought, and took a deep hit off her bottle. Then she screwed the top of the bottle back on, banged her chest with the heel of her hand, and proceeded on her way home.

Lenny sat at her dressing table staring into a mirror as she rubbed some of Old Grandmama's aging creme into her hands. The smell of the lotion brought Old Grandmama back to her. A tough old bird, everyone had called the woman. Much tougher than Old Grandaddy. She was the sort who believed that to spare the rod was to spoil the child. So there was no nonsense tolerated in her home. No crying over dead mothers. Nothing like that. You accepted the burdens the Lord put on your back and you carried them with perfect grace.

Old Grandmama had never liked the way Lenny slouched. She'd back Lenny against a wall and push her shoulders against the plaster. "Even a homely girl can hold her head up high," Old Grandmama would say, "and I should know because I used to be one. We're a lot alike, Lenora."

And now Lenny could see the resemblance in the mirror, could trace the sags under her own eyes just as she used to be able to trace the ones under Old Grandmama's.

The month Old Grandmama lay dying, she had given Lenny the key to her bureau. "You can have my clothes, Lenora. When I'm dust, they're yours."

"But they don't fit me," Lenny had protested, though really what she had wanted to say was that they were too old and worn.

Old Grandmama had smiled. "Oh they'll fit

you soon enough, girl. Don't you worry about that."

And Old Grandmama had been right. These days, more than half the clothes Lenny wore were ones from that locked bureau.

Lenny glanced down at herself. The night-clothes she wore were from that bureau. Babe had wrinkled her nose when she had seen Lenny putting them on. "I like lace and things," Babe had said. "Myself, I don't like wearing the clothes of a corpse."

"But don't you see how her things fit me?" Lenny had asked.

"No," Babe had said sadly. "No, that's not what I see at all."

Now Lenny sighed and turned away from her mirror. Babe was sitting on her little bed setting her hair. The nightclothes she wore were frilly and girllike. Lenny looked at Babe's baby-doll pajamas and tried to picture herself wearing something similar. No. The very idea was ludicrous, like a chimp in party clothes.

Suddenly the bedroom door opened and Meg walked in the room carrying the newspaper. Lenny pointedly ignored Meg's presence, but Babe glanced up and smiled.

"Hello," Meg said nervously.

"Hi, Meg," Babe replied.

Lenny closed her bottle of hand creme and began buffing away at her nails. Meg eyed her for a moment, then walked over to Babe. "Here's your paper."

Babe tossed down her hair rollers and grabbed the paper enthusiastically. With a wide grin on her face, she opened the paper to the front page and read the headline. "Oh here it is," she said admiringly, "right on the front page!" And Babe quickly scooted off her bed and hurried over to a drawer for a pair of scissors and some glue. Soon she was happily snipping away at the front page of the paper as though she was clipping out an article about how she had been given a good citizen award or a beauty contest title.

Meg looked Lenny's way again, but Lenny kept her eyes on her nails, so Meg sighed and lit a cigarette. For a time, the only sounds in the room were those of Babe slicing away at her paper and Meg blowing great whooshes of smoke from her mouth. But finally Meg couldn't take the silence anymore and spun toward Lenny.

"All right!" she yelled. "I *lied*!" And then, quietly, "I couldn't help it. When I saw how tired and sick Old Grandaddy's gotten, those stories, they just flew out. All I wanted to see was him smiling and happy."

Lenny continued to ignore Meg, but Babe turned to her sympathetically. "Oh, Meg, he *is* sick, isn't he?"

Meg went over to Babe. "Why, he's gotten all white and milky; he's almost evaporated!"

All of a sudden Lenny stood up and looked at Meg with painful, furious eyes: "But still you shouldn't have lied! It was just wrong for you to tell such lies."

Thankful that at least Lenny had stopped pretending she didn't exist, Meg ran to her: "Well, I know that! Don't you think I *know* that?"

Lenny shrugged and glanced away from Meg

again, but Meg pressed up close to her, forcing Lenny to look back. "I hate myself when I lie for that old man. I do," she insisted, breathing bourbon on Lenny's face. "I feel so weak. And then I have to go and do at least three or four things that I know he'd despise just to get even with that miserable, old, bossy man!"

"Oh, Meg, please don't talk so about Old Grandaddy," Lenny said frantically. "It sounds so ungrateful." And as though she were quoting from the Bible: "Why, he went out of his way to make a home for us. All he ever wanted was the best for us."

"Well, I guess it was," Meg said, feeling hopeless because she knew there was some truth to Lenny's words. "Only sometimes I wonder what we wanted."

Babe, who had finished clipping out her article and was now getting an old photo album from her suitcase, looked up at her sisters thoughtfully. "Well, one thing *I* wanted was a team of white horses to ride Mama's coffin to her grave." And tossing the album onto her bed: "That's one thing I wanted."

Lenny and Meg exchanged glances while Babe sat down and began gluing her news article into the album. Finally Lenny spoke. "Really, Babe, I don't understand why you have to put in the articles that are about the unhappy things in your life. Why would you want to remember them?"

Babe shrugged. "I don't know. I just like an accurate record, I suppose."

Lenny winced. She knew that Babe had articles about Mama in the album. How in the world a person could keep clippings like those about Mama side by side with pictures of senior prom and so forth, Lenny didn't have the vaguest idea.

Babe rubbed her article carefully into the album and then began flipping pages. Her eyes went quickly over pictures of herself from babyhood through high school graduation, and then stopped at a photo of Zackery eating wedding cake. Bits and pieces of frosting dotted his chin like mosquito-bite lotion, and slurps of red wine lay on the shirtfront of his white tuxedo. What a pig, Babe thought, and turned her attention to another picture. "Look," she called over to her sisters, "here's a picture of me when I got married."

"Let's see," Meg said, hurrying over to the album with Lenny at her heels.

Lenny grinned at the photograph. There was Babe out on the dance floor, spinning round and round in her long white gown. A net veil sailed about her head, giving the picture a hazy, dreamlike quality. "My word," Lenny whispered, "you look about twelve years old."

"I was just eighteen."

Meg stared at the picture and remembered Babe's reception. How Doc had wanted her to try to catch the bouquet. How she had said Lenny should be the one to get married next. Doc had shaken his head. "You wait for Lenny, you might die single." Doc and Meg had both laughed—it was just a joke—but then they'd heard a muffled kind of cry and turned to see Lenny running from the room. They hadn't known she'd been standing near them, hadn't meant for her to hear. Meg ran after Lenny and tried to explain Doc had only been teasing, but it did no good. Lenny stood in a bathroom crying, saying over and over, "But he's right. He is absolutely right."

Meg tried to turn her thoughts away from Lenny. Thinking about Lenny was like thinking about starvation in the third world or something. All it did was make you feel horribly depressed and guilty. So she pointed to the picture of Babe and said, "You're smiling. Were you happy then?"

Babe laughed. "Well, I was drunk on champagne punch. I do remember that."

Lenny looked at another photograph, one she herself had taken. "Oh, there's Meg singing at Greeny's."

In the picture, Meg stood under a spotlight, her eyes glowing, her skin radiant. Meg's first night at Greeny's. The whole family had come to see her. Lenny hadn't known what to expect; all she had ever heard Meg singing were songs from the radio which Meg hollered out while showering. So it had shocked Lenny that when Meg walked out on the stage and began to sing, what came from her lips were magical sounds. She had felt so proud of Meg that night, had wanted so desperately to capture some of that magic in a picture.

Now she looked at the picture carefully for a time, then took Meg's hand and quietly said, "You're so beautiful."

Babe nodded. "Yes, you are. You're beautiful."

But Meg couldn't bear to glance at the picture, much less hear her sisters' praise. She turned away from the album and felt something tighten in her heart. "Oh stop," she told Lenny and Babe. "I'm not."

Tears started to form in Meg's eyes. Lenny, seeing them, poked Babe. "Look," she said, wishing she could put her sister back on Greeny's stage again, "Meg's starting to cry."

"Oh, Meg," Babe whispered.

Meg blinked her eyes rapidly. "I'm not . . ."

"Quick!" Babe said. "Better turn the page. We don't want Meg crying." And she snapped over to the next page of the album to a faded photograph of a handsome young man strutting playfully along a beach.

"Why, it's Daddy," Lenny said after a moment.

Meg touched her father's picture gingerly. "Where'd you get that picture, Babe? I thought she'd burned them all."

"Ah, I just found it around," Babe said, though the truth of the matter was that she had reached into the fireplace after one of Mama's purgings and lifted out not only a photograph of her father but also a slightly charred shoe of his.

Lenny took the picture from the album and turned it around. "What does it say here? What's that inscription?" But she couldn't make out the smudges of her mother's raked handwriting.

Babe knew the inscription by heart. "It says, 'Jimmy clowning on the beach, 1956.' "

"Well, will you look at that smile," Lenny said, wondering how a man as glamorous as her father could have sired someone as plain as herself.

Meg whistled. "Jesus. Those white teeth."

And to Babe: "Turn the page, will you? We can't do any worse than this!"

Babe stuck her father's picture back in the album and flipped a page ahead.

Suddenly all three sisters gasped. Directly before their eyes was a large, yellowed photograph clipped from a newspaper of two bodies—one notably smaller than the other—wrapped in police tarp cloths.

A shiver went down Lenny's spine as Babe whispered, "It's Mama and the cat."

"Oh turn the page . . ." Lenny begged, but no one could. Instead the sisters stared and stared at the picture of their mother and her pet cat.

Meg was the first to look away. She glanced at a photograph on the facing page. It was also of her mother, but of her mother alive. Taken a week before her death, the photograph showed a thin woman, strange and hollow, peeling potatoes out on the back porch steps of her home in Vicksburg. She didn't seem to be looking at anything, just staring blankly at a world that had long since lost its sparkle for her.

Babe and Lenny couldn't take their eyes off the newspaper clipping. But while Lenny focused on the larger of the two covered bodies—her mother's—Babe looked at the smaller body—the cat's. Finally Babe spoke. "That old yellow cat. You know, I bet if she hadn't've hung that old cat with her, she wouldn't have gotten all that national coverage."

Meg winced. If Babe said another word, she just knew she was going to have to run to her bourbon and chug down the rest of the contents in the bottle. "Why are we talking about this?" she asked.

"Meg's right," Lenny said. "It was so sad."

"It was awfully sad," Babe agreed.

Still, no one could turn the page or the conversation. And finally, Lenny—usually the first to keep talk away from the subject of Mama—gulped hard and whispered, "I remember how we all three just sat up on that bed the day of the service, all dressed up in our black velveteen suits, crying the whole morning long."

Everyone looked at Meg's bed and recalled that horrible morning. Babe had been in charge of handing tissues to her older sisters and had run from room to room in the house searching for more boxes of Kleenex after she and Lenny and Meg had used up the one in their bedroom. Then Old Grandaddy had come to them, a Camel cigarette in his hand, all dressed up and trying his best to be cheerful. "Hush all this crying, chillun," he had said. "Old Grandaddy's gonna take you out for some breakfast. Whatever you want—you gonna have it."

Off they had gone to a diner on the square. Lenny, fourteen years old and trying to act proper, had started to order something sensible, like scrambled eggs, but Meg and Babe had insisted on banana splits. So that's what all three girls ordered, much to the waitress's surprise. And every time they would finish one, Old Grandaddy had shouted for another to be brought. "Looks like you need some more slivers of nuts," he had told Meg. And then, shouting to the waitress as though it were the

Fourth of July: "Bring this little lady a plate of some of those nut slivers!"

Babe began to giggle. "Banana splits for breakfast! I think I ate about five!" She had asked Old Grandaddy not to let the waitress put any pineapple topping on her ice cream, so he had told the woman to give Babe a king-size bowl of chocolate syrup, which Babe had proceeded to hurl all over her sundae.

"God, we were so sick," Meg said, starting to laugh a little.

"Oh, we were," Lenny agreed.

Meg pointed at Lenny. "Your face turned green."

Lenny nodded. "I was just sick as a dog."

Old Grandaddy had kept the girls at the diner all morning. He had sat drinking coffee and telling funny stories to them. Anything to keep their minds off the day to come. Then they had gone home to Old Grandmama, who took one look at the girls' nauseous faces and the ice cream stains on their brand-new funeral suits and proceeded to lay into Old Grandaddy with a vengeance.

"Old Grandmama was furious," Babe said, remembering how she had chased Old Grandaddy around the house with a thick, heavy Bible poised like a weapon. Old Grandaddy had had to keep moving pretty fast to keep from being struck down by God's words.

Meg sighed. "The thing about Old Grandaddy is he keeps trying to make us happy and we end up getting stomachaches and throwing up in the flower arrangements."

"Oh that was me!" Babe giggled, recalling

how the combination of banana splits in her stomach and the smell of chrysanthemums in her nose had proved too much for her at the funeral parlor. "I threw up in the flowers! Oh no! How embarrassing!"

Lenny laughed and reached out for Babe's blond curls. "Oh, Babe . . ."

Feeling Lenny's warm hand on her head, Babe turned around. Both of her sisters were looking at her with so much love, so much hope. She threw her arms around them. "Oh, Lenny! Oh, Meg!"

Meg felt her eyes starting to mist over again. But this time she didn't even try to keep the tears back. She squeezed both Lenny and Babe as tight as she could. "Oh Babe! Oh Lenny! It's so good to be home."

For a time the three sisters held to each other, Meg's and Lenny's grudges against each other gone, Babe's predicament forgotten. They were together again, in each other's arms and hearts, and all their differences and misunderstandings were nothing compared to the fact that they were sisters who wanted no more from each other than the love they knew they had.

Suddenly Lenny jumped up with excitement. "Hey! I have an idea."

"What?" asked Babe.

"Let's play cards!"

"Oh, let's do!" Babe replied happily, remembering all the Friday nights she and Meg and Lenny had sat at the kitchen table playing cards until Babe had finally dropped off to sleep past midnight and had to be carried to bed by her two older sisters.

Even Meg was excited by the suggestion. "All *right*!" she shouted.

Lenny was thrilled. Everything was going to be as it once was. "Oh good!" she said."It'll be just like when we used to sit around playing Hearts all night long."

Babe hopped up from her bed. "I know," she said as she hurried toward the bedroom door, "I'll go down and fix us up some popcorn!"

Meg ran after her. "And hot chocolate," she called out, remembering how she had always won at hearts when she had her trusty cup of hot chocolate and lost miserably when she hadn't. "Don't forget the hot chocolate."

Lenny scurried off after both Meg and Babe. Her face glowed with pleasure. So many years she'd been living in the house with just Old Grandaddy for company. And all he ever did at night was lock himself in the bathroom with back issues of his beloved *National Geographic* magazines.

The sisters ran through the house, laughing with excitement, freed from all the problems of their grown-up lives, magically transformed into giddy teenagers.

"Now let's see," Lenny said when they reached the kitchen. "I think I have a deck of cards here somewhere."

While Lenny rummaged through various drawers, Babe and Meg tore through cabinets in search of popcorn and cocoa mix. The kitchen soon was bursting with activity as the sisters hurried about, bumping into one another, in an effort to get everything perfectly set up for their big game of Hearts. Everything was to be exactly as it once was.

Babe poured oil and popping corn into a big pot. Boy, I love hearts, she thought. Boy, I really and truly do. And then: Unfortunately, I don't have the foggiest recollection as to how to play Hearts. Out loud she said, "I hope I can remember all the rules. Are hearts good or bad?"

Meg searched through her own memory. "Bad, I think. Aren't they, Lenny?"

"That's right," Lenny replied. "Hearts are bad, but the Black Sister is the worst of all."

The game was slowly starting to come back to Meg. "Oh, that's right!" she shouted, pouring milk and cocoa mix into a pot. "And the Black Sister is the Queen of Spades."

But Babe still wasn't clear in her head. "And spades are the black cards that aren't the puppy-dog feet?"

Meg thought about that for a moment. "Right," she said finally. "And she counts a lot of points."

"And points are bad?" Babe asked.

"Right," Meg replied.

And so the sisters continued with their preparations, Meg and Babe confident that Lenny would eventually recall the finer points of the game for them.

Lenny, still searching for her deck of cards, felt happier than she had in years. After Babe and Meg had moved away from home, she had sometimes sat in the kitchen playing Solitaire, but all that had done was to make her nostalgic for times with her sisters. Plus, she had hated playing a game called Solitaire—it had made her all the more painfully aware of how alone in the world she was. So she had put her playing cards away with the thought that never again would she use them. But now here she was with her sisters, a part of a *family* again.

Her hot chocolate started up on the stove, Meg went over to a message pad near the telephone. "I'll get some paper so we can keep score." But no sooner had she said that than the phone began to ring. "I'll get it," she told Lenny.

Lenny nodded and opened a junk drawer. There were the cards! She lifted them out of the drawer with triumph. "Here they are!" she called out to her sisters.

Meg smiled and picked up the phone. "Hello . . . No, this is Meg Magrath."

"Why, look at these cards," Lenny whispered to Babe. They're *years* old."

"Let me see," Babe whispered back, and went over to the kitchen table where she and Lenny proceeded to note the various chocolate and oil stains on the cards as they eavesdropped on Meg's conversation.

"*Doc!*" Meg cried out with delight. "How *are* you?"

Lenny quickly looked over at her sister. Meg was positively glowing with pleasure.

"You're where?" Meg was saying. And then, with what seemed to Lenny to be extreme eagerness: "Well sure! Yeah, come right on over."

Suddenly, Lenny took the cards back from Babe and began shuffling them rapidly. All the pleasure she had felt moments before was dissolving into bitterness as Meg chattered on with Doc.

By the time Meg hung up, both Lenny and Babe were staring at her. She grinned at them and tried to sound casual. "That was Doc Porter. He's down the street at Al's Grill. He's gonna come over."

"He is?" Lenny asked coolly as Meg ran to a mirror and began fixing her hair.

"He said he wanted to come and see me," Meg said, smiling into the mirror as she tried her hardest to give her hair a kind of sexy aura.

"Oh," Lenny said quietly.

Babe sighed and went back to her popcorn making, leaving Lenny at the table shuffling the cards faster and faster and faster. At last Lenny paused in her shuffling and turned to Meg. "Well, do you still want to play?"

"No," Meg said, now applying some lipstick, "I don't think so."

Lenny tried not to sound angry. "All right." But after a moment she had to say something more. "You know, it's really not much fun playing Hearts with only two people."

"I'm sorry," Meg said offhandedly. "Maybe after Doc leaves I'll join you."

Lenny decided to try one more time to be nice: "I know; maybe Doc'll want to play, then we can have a game of bridge."

But Meg instantly vetoed the suggestion. "I don't think so. Doc never liked cards. Maybe we'll just go out somewhere."

Lenny let the cards flutter down to the table. Meg was lighting a cigarette and moving around the kitchen with happy expectation. "Meg . . ." Lenny began delicately.

Meg didn't even look at her, but instead answered in a rather preoccupied-with-anticipated-pleasure sort of tone. "What?"

"Well, Doc's married now."

"I know," Meg said lightly. "You told me."

"Oh, well, as long as you know that," Lenny told her. And then, a little more pointedly: "As long as you *know* that."

Meg walked over to an extremely strange piece of modern pottery. "Yes, I know," she said, ashing her cigarette in the middle of the clay-piece. "She made the pot."

Suddenly Lenny rose from the table and approached Meg. "Ah, could I . . . could I ask you something?"

"What?"

Lenny swallowed hard and tried to make her voice come out as steady as possible. "I just wanted to ask you . . ."

"What?"

Lenny's mouth stayed open, but no more words followed. And then, too hurt, scared, and furious to confront Meg about Doc, she ran from the room to the screened-in porch, where she grabbed her birthday candy with a vengeance and returned to Meg. "Well, just why did you take one little bite out of each piece of candy in this box and then just put it back in?"

"Oh," Meg said, a bit embarrassed to see the mess she had made of Lenny's candy. "Well, I was looking for ones with nuts."

Lenny stared at Meg with horror. "The ones with *nuts*?"

"Yeah."

"But there *are* none with *nuts*. It's a box of

assorted *cremes,*" Lenny shouted, flashing the label on the box in Meg's face. "All it has in it are *cremes*!"

"Oh."

Now Lenny turned the box toward herself. Her voice starting to break and whine, she continued with her tirade. "It says right here on the box 'Assorted Cremes,' not nuts! Besides, this was my one and only birthday present to me. My *only one*!"

Meg, alarmed by Lenny's overreaction, looked away and said, "I'm sorry. I'll get you another box."

That wasn't good enough for Lenny. Truly ranting now, she screamed out, "I don't *want* another box! That's not the point!"

"What is the point?" Meg asked quietly.

Suddenly Lenny was at a loss for words. What was the point? She couldn't even be sure. All she knew was that somehow, some way, Meg had ruined her entire existence. But the point? "I don't know . . . it's . . . it's . . ." And then inspiration came to Lenny. "It's that you have no respect for other people's property! You just take whatever you want. Why, remember how you always had layers and layers of jingle bells sewed onto your petticoats while Babe and I only had three apiece?"

Meg turned to Babe with an exasperated look on her face. "Oh God! She's starting up about those stupid jingle bells."

"Well," Lenny said icily, "it's a specific example of how you always got what you wanted."

Meg stubbed out her cigarette and looked

Lenny keenly in the eyes. "Oh come on. You're just upset because Doc called."

For a brief moment Lenny felt as though Meg had just shot her between the eyes. But then she recovered. "Who said anything about Doc?" And then bitterly: "Why, I've long since given up worrying about you and all your men."

Now it was Meg's turn to be devastated. Spinning toward Lenny with fury, she said, "Look. I *know* I've had too many men. Believe me, I've had *way* too many men. But it's not my fault you haven't had *any,* or maybe just that one from Memphis."

Babe looked up from the stove with terror as Lenny, suddenly stricken with shock, quietly asked, "What one from Memphis?"

Meg swallowed. She knew she had gone too far, had betrayed both of her sisters with one slip of the mouth. But now there was no way back. Unable to look at either Babe or Lenny, she slowly said, "The one Babe told me about. From the . . . club."

Lenny's eyes went huge with betrayal and she turned quickly to her youngest sister. *"Babe!"* But all Babe did was spin equally quickly to her middle sister: *"Meg!"*

Now all three sisters were fighting.

"How could you!" Lenny shouted to Babe. "I asked you not to tell anyone! I'm so ashamed! Who else have you told? Did you tell anyone else?"

Babe ignored Lenny's questions out of guilty embarrassment and instead ran to Meg. Furiously she cried out, "Why'd you have to open your big mouth?"

"How was I supposed to know?" Meg shouted back. "You never said not to tell anyone!"

Meg's answer only infuriated Babe more. "Can't you use your head just for once!" And then, turning to Lenny with great, contrite apologies: "No, I never told anyone else. Somehow it just slipped out to Meg. Really. It just *flew* out of my mouth."

But Lenny was already starting to cry. She looked at Babe with sorrowful, angry eyes. "I'll never, never, *never* be able to trust you again." And with those words out, she ran from her sisters and tore up the stairway.

Babe and Meg instantly took off after her."Oh, for heaven's sake, Lenny!" Meg yelled, thundering up the steps two at a time. "We were just worried about you! We wanted to find a way to make you happy!"

Lenny didn't even bother to turn around. Racing along the upstairs corridor, she shrieked out, "Happy! *Happy!* I'll *never* be happy!"

"Well, not if you keep living your life as Old Grandaddy's nursemaid," Meg yelled back.

For her response, Lenny hurried into the sisters' bedroom and slammed the door with all her might.

Meg started to go after Lenny, but Babe blocked her way. "Meg, shut up!"

"I can't help it!" Meg said, and burst into the room after Lenny. "I just know,"she told her sobbing sister, "that the reason you stopped seeing this man from Memphis was because of Old Grandaddy."

Lenny looked up from her bed. "What? Babe didn't tell you the rest of the story."

"Oh, she said it was something about your shrunken ovary."

"Meg!" shrieked Babe.

Lenny turned to Babe with an aghast expression: *"Babe!"*

Babe ran to Lenny for forgiveness. "I just *mentioned* it."

Now Meg, too, went over to Lenny. "But I don't believe a word of that story."

Lenny shook her head with indignation. "Oh I don't care what you believe! It's so easy for you . . . you always have men falling in love with you." And then, letting herself slide into despair: "But I have this underdeveloped ovary and I can't have any children and my hair is falling out in the comb . . . so what man can love me? What man's gonna love me?"

"A lot of men," Meg cried out passionately.

Babe wrapped her arms around her big sister. "Yeah, a lot! A *whole* lot!"

"Old Grandaddy's the only one who seems to think otherwise," Meg added.

" 'Cause he doesn't want to see me rejected and humiliated," Lenny said, her tears continuing to fall.

It infuriated Meg to see Lenny succumb to Old Grandaddy's self-serving notions. Why Lenny had to obey the man and believe everything he told her baffled her almost as much as why she herself had to put on the dog for him and try to fulfill all his dreams. "Oh come on now, Lenny," she said. "Don't be so pathetic. Just tell me. Did you actually ask that man from Memphis all about this?"

Lenny tried to stop crying. She wiped at her

nose, squeezed her eyes rapidly, and took a breath. "No, I didn't," she began, "because I . . ." And then she broke apart, and her body started shaking with sobs. "I just didn't want him not to want me. . . ."

Meg's heart ached to watch Lenny in so much pain. She reached her hand toward Lenny's shoulder. "Lenny . . ."

But Lenny didn't want Meg's sympathy and pulled away from her. "Don't talk to me anymore! I just think I'm gonna vomit. I just hope all this doesn't cause me to vomit!" And covering her hands over her mouth, Lenny tore out of the bedroom for the bathroom.

Babe hurried after Lenny, but Meg stayed behind in the bedroom, furious and guilty and just *dying* to have a drink.

Eight

Half an hour later, Meg was sitting on the front steps of the house with a bottle of Old Crow at her lips. Only the snoopiest of Hazlehurst's citizenry remained out on their porches to see her red eyes and mascara-smeared cheeks. But even those who could see her weren't able to look into her heart and understand what was breaking her down. Even she herself couldn't do that. Why she had to lay into Lenny, she had no idea. It only made her miserable and full of aches. And giving away Babe's secret about Charlie in Memphis was totally wretched and unforgivable.

All that was clear to Meg was that she was on a downhill course and couldn't seem to stop herself from hitting lower. But when had it all started? Was her present misery just the natural result of living too hard and fast and cocky? Was there some sort of spiteful God up in the sky who spat down periodically on girls who wanted to be singing stars? Well, if there was, Meg presumed he was happy now—had been happy since Christmas when Meg had found herself incapable of singing in a bathroom, let alone on a stage.

Suddenly, Meg heard the roar of a pickup truck and she shuddered. It was Doc coming, she knew it. And what bad thing, she wondered, was she about to do now? She could feel herself already giving in to temptation without even having to see his face. A kind of reckless, hopeful thing was coming over her, the same sort of thing that had sent her tearing off to Hollywood, the same sort of thing that had eventually led to her losing her voice. . . .

Meg took another slug off her bottle as Doc's truck came into view, then she pulled her blue-jean jacket over her shoulders and watched Doc coming toward her. Her heart pounded and she found herself smiling like crazy. Here was someone who hadn't seemed to have gotten any older or sadder since she'd last seen him. He was still her handsome, steady Doc. And he looked happy to see her, too.

"Well Doc," she called out gently. "Well, it's Doc."

Doc walked over to the steps and grinned at her. "So Meggy . . . you're home."

"Yeah, I've come on home. I've come on home to see about Babe."

Doc nodded and gave Meg a long, steady gaze which she returned. But out loud all he said was, "And how's Babe?"

"Fine," Meg replied without thinking. And then, recalling that Babe might be about to serve a life sentence in prison, added, "Well, fair. She's fair."

Doc nodded again. To his eyes, Meg was even more beautiful than she had been when he'd last seen her in Biloxi. She'd been a girl then—headstrong, wild, and bursting with gutsy passions, maybe—but still just a girl. Now, the person in front of him was a woman. Her posture, her eyes, even her smile, had grown up. He could also tell she had been knocked around by life, that she was going through sea-changes.

"Hey, you wanna drink?" Meg asked.

"Sure, whatcha got?"

"Bourbon."

Meg handed the bottle to Doc. He took a long swallow, then handed it back to her. She grinned and took a great slug, too.

"So . . ." Doc began, his eyes sliding from her face down to her long, lean legs. "Wanna go for a ride in the country and look at the moon?"

For a moment, Meg let her gaze also slide downward. To Doc's shoulders. His chest. His waist . . . She glanced back up at his eyes. He was staring at her. She stared back for some time. Then he reached out his hand and they walked slowly to his truck.

As soon as they were driving along, windows open, hair blowing in the night wind, Meg felt her spirits soaring. They didn't talk to each other at first, just drove toward the familiar country roads outside town that they had always liked to ride along. Meg watched the night get darker and darker as they left the lit houses and stores of Hazlehurst behind, and soon the headlights on Doc's truck were the only lights she could see anywhere.

The truck rolled over red-dirt roads. Meg breathed in the cool, clean air of southern country in springtime and looked out her window at huge pine trees flying past her. She laughed out loud and turned on the radio.

Soon she and Doc were both grinning, keeping time to the songs on the radio, and passing the bourbon bottle back and forth. The moon sailed ahead of them in the sky. Everything was just as it once had been between them—except, of course, for the fact that Doc was married now. To a Yankee. Who had given him Yankee-style children.

"So how's your wife?" Meg asked pleasantly.

"She's . . . fine."

Meg took a long drink, and then said, "I hear ya got two kids."

"Yeah," Doc said slowly. "Yeah, I got two kids."

"A boy and a girl?"

"That's right, Meggy, a boy and a girl."

Meg nodded. "Well, that's what you always said you wanted, wasn't it?"

Doc looked at her. "Is that what I said?" he asked quietly. And then he turned his attention back to the road and Meg turned to the pine trees again.

They drove in silence to the place where they had always parked and necked in high school, a beautiful section of land overlooking the river. Meg chewed at her nails and smoked—anything but think about what was or was not to come.

At last they arrived at the scene of their younger passions. Meg leaped from the truck and went around to the front. Leaning against the hood, she looked out toward the river. Doc sat in the truck a few moments more, watching her, then went to her.

"Well, it's been a long time," he said at last.

Meg glanced from the river to Doc. "It *has* been a long time."

"Let's see . . ." Doc began. "When was the last time we saw each other?"

Meg shrugged nervously. The last thing she wanted to do was go through the hurricane ordeal with him. "I can't quite recall," she said in a bit, fumbling for a cigarette.

Quite aware of Meg's edginess, Doc smiled to himself slyly. "Wasn't it in Biloxi?" he asked innocently.

"Ah, Biloxi," Meg said with much forced casualness. "I believe so."

Doc leaned toward her and pressed on. "And wasn't there a . . . a hurricane going on at the time?"

"Was there?" Meg asked, lighting her cigarette with trembling hands but still managing to keep her voice steady.

"Yes there was, one hell of a hurricane. Cordelia, I believe they called it. Hurricane Cordelia."

Meg looked to the river again. "Yes, now I remember. It was a *beautiful* hurricane." And it truly had been to Meg's way of thinking. The ocean crashing against buildings, the wind sending trees soaring like strange kites through the dark, fast-moving sky. It all would have been so perfect if a restaurant hadn't fallen on Doc's leg.

"We had quite a time down there," Doc was saying. "Drinking vodka, eating oysters on the half shell, dancing all night long. And the wind was blowing."

"Oh, God, was it blowing."

"*Goddamn* was it blowing."

"There never *has* been such a wind blowing."

Suddenly Doc turned away and wiped his hands across his face. "Oh God, Meggy," he said. "Oh God . . ."

Meg turned to him, her heart swollen. "I know Doc. It was my fault to leave you. I was crazy." And then, trying to put into words a feeling she'd had deep inside her ever since the day she'd found Mama and the cat, "I felt choked!"

Doc shook his head sadly. "I felt like a fool."

"No."

Doc looked at her, his eyes full of long-ago questions. "I just kept wondering why."

"I don't know why," Meg said quietly. She tried to rethink the day. She'd been drinking since early in the morning. Doc had kept saying they should clear out, the city was being evacuated. Around them, everyone was getting in cars, driving away, taking to school and church basements, boarding up their windows and hiding down in cellars. Meg had wanted to wait out the storm. She'd enjoyed the feeling of being half blown off the ground. But Doc had insisted they should go, had started carrying her off to his truck. Laughing, teasing, she'd promised to marry him if he'd wait out the hurricane with her. . . . "I didn't want to care," Meg said at last, remembering Doc pinned beneath the debris of the restaurant's dance floor, his face so scared and full of need. "I *did* care though. I did."

Doc eyed Meg for a long time, then sighed. "Ah . . . hell." And he walked off from the truck, over to the bank of the river. He watched the rushing water below him for a time, then glanced over at Meg with a smile. What was the use of going back over all of that? It was done. He was married. A husband and father. "You still singing those sad songs?"

"No," Meg said.

"Why not?"

Meg shrugged and walked over to the riverbank to stand beside Doc. "I don't know. Things got worse for me. After a while, I just couldn't sing anymore. I tell you, I had one hell of a time over Christmas."

"What do you mean?"

"I went nuts," Meg said, the words sounding strange and foreign to her own ears. This was the first time she had told anybody about her "Christmas adventure," and she didn't know how she was supposed to talk about the experience, let alone how she was supposed to feel. "Ended up in L.A. County Hospital. Psychiatric ward."

"Ah, hell, Meggy," Doc said gently. "What happened?"

Meg shrugged. "I don't really know. I couldn't sing anymore, so I lost my job. All I could do was sit around in chairs, chewing on my fingers." She had had a toothache. A raging, head-banging toothache. But she couldn't even think of leaving her apartment anymore. Instead she'd just sat with her toothache, letting the pain flow through her, for days. . . . "Then one afternoon I ran screaming out of the apartment with all my money and jewelry and valuables and tried to stuff it all into one of those March of Dime collection boxes. That was when they nabbed me." She smiled at Doc. "Sad story. Meg goes mad."

Doc stared at Meg for a time. The moon was shining on her eyes, making them flicker with strange, magical light. He reached out for her softly, pressed her closely to his chest and held her firm. "God," he whispered, "there sure is a moon out tonight."

Meg held tightly to Doc's shoulders, breathed in his scent. "Is there?" And then she looked up at his face, his taut jaw, his deep, thoughtful eyes.

Slowly Doc moved his head down to hers and kissed her full on the mouth. Meg shivered and pulled away. "I don't know," she whispered, her heart pounding with anticipation. "I don't wanna start up. It'll be too hard if we start up."

Doc smiled. "Who says we're gonna start up? We're just looking at the moon. For one night just you and me are taking a ride in the country and looking out at the moon."

"One night? Looking out at the moon?"

Doc grinned. "You got it."

Meg closed her eyes and started laughing—a throaty, song-filled happy laugh, the kind of laugh she hadn't known how to laugh in years. "Well," she said at last, her heart soaring, her eyes opening to the floating dream of a milk-white moon, "all right."

* * *

Meanwhile the same glowing moon that was shining on Meg was pouring its light through the windows of the Magrath house and casting long shadows in the sisters' bedroom, where Lenny lay sleeping away the last remaining hours of June's first day.

Babe, unable to sleep, crept along in moonlight to Old Grandaddy's library with her golden saxophone. After closing the door carefully behind her, she carried the sax over toward the brightest window of the room. Dressed only in a lacy slip, she stood at the window for a time, her fingers caressing the saxophone as though it were a long-awaited lover.

The saxophone glittered in the night. Babe looked at it with awe—it was so big, so elaborately curved, so powerful. To touch your mouth to such a thing was a thrill in itself, just to know your lips were pressing the same kind of reed once blessed by someone who had actually known how to play the thing.

Babe put the instrument to her mouth and blew with all the strength her tiny body could muster. The saxophone let loose with a screeching flood of noise that shocked Babe. Her eyes widened with fear, but also with a delicious ecstasy, for the shrill, awful scream coming from her golden sax was the very sound she'd been trying to free from her soul since her wedding night.

She sucked in her breath again, this time even longer and deeper than the first, and blew once more. Now the sound that hurled out of her instrument was passionate in its agony. Babe reveled in the saxophone's scream and was about to blow again when she heard a loud, urgent knock at the front door, followed by Barnette's call: "Becky! Becky, is that you?"

Babe set her saxophone down and went running happily to the living room. There, she grabbed a raincoat from a closet, put it on, then hurried to the door.

Barnette stood at the threshold of the door for a moment with eyes that were obviously troubled and haunted even though his smile showed how happy he was to see his dear, beloved Becky.

Babe grinned at him. "Hello, Barnette. Come on in."

Barnette walked slowly into the living room. "Look, I, ah, I met with Zackery over at the hospital."

"Oh?"

"It seems . . . Well, it seems his sister, Lucille, was somewhat suspicious."

"Suspicious?" Babe asked nervously.

Barnette nodded. "She hired a private detective."

Babe grimaced. So *that* explained why a man in a dark suit had seemed to be turning up in the most unlikely places—at her beauty parlor, in various women's bathrooms in restaurants. . . .

With great reluctance, Barnette handed Babe a small envelope. She took it even more reluctantly, then began looking at photographs of herself and Willie Jay. There they were, fully nude, out in the garage at the Botrelle mansion.

Barnette swallowed as he watched Babe's stricken, hopeless face. "They were taken about two weeks ago," he said quietly. "It seems she wasn't going to show them to Botrelle straight away. She, ah, wanted to wait till the time was right."

Babe glanced up at Barnette slowly as she put the photos back into the envelope. "These are pictures of Willie Jay and me," she explained, "out in the garage."

"I know," Barnette replied, turning red in the face.

Babe gasped. "You *looked* at these pictures?"

"I . . . well . . . professionally I looked at them," Barnette said hoarsely.

Babe was beside herself. Just the thought of Barnette seeing her doing the various things the photographs showed her doing with Willie Jay made her want to drop dead on the spot. "Oh mercy!" she cried out. "Oh mercy!" And then, racing toward the kitchen with the pictures, "Well, we can burn them, can't we? Quick, we can burn them."

Barnette shook his head sadly. "It won't do any good. They have the negatives."

Babe stopped in her tracks, then slammed her body helplessly into a large, wooden desk. "Oh no!" she shouted out with despair. And then, not knowing what else to do, she began crashing against furniture around the room, banging into chairs and hurling them over onto the floor in a hopeless, blind fit.

Barnette ran after her, worried that she might hurt herself. "There, there, now," he said as soothingly as he could.

But Babe couldn't be comforted. Eluding his

grasp, she ran about the room, her cries and bangs getting louder: "Oh no, oh no, oh *no*!"

Suddenly, from the upstairs bedroom, came a call from Lenny: "Babe! Are you all right?"

Babe froze in horror.

"Babe?"

Babe glanced down at the envelope as she heard the upstairs bedroom door open. What was she ever going to do if Lenny saw the pictures? In terror she rushed at a bookshelf in the room and began leaping up at it in an attempt to hide the photographs on top of the shelf.

Barnette, hearing Lenny's approaching footsteps, ran to Babe's aid. He lifted her up high over the bookshelf.

"I'm all right!" Babe yelled to Lenny as she dropped the photographs on the top shelf. "Go on back to bed!"

But Lenny didn't go back to bed. Instead she appeared on the steps, dressed in one of Old Grandmama's robes, her face lost in smears of white night cream. "What's the matter?" she was asking. "What's going on down here?"

"Nothin'!" Babe called out, but it was too late. Lenny was now at the bottom of the stairs and was staring in shock at Barnette and Babe. What in the world was Babe's lawyer doing holding her up in the air?

Barnette instantly let Babe down as Lenny eyed him with shock while Babe began leaping about the room like a ballerina gone mad.

"We're . . . we're just dancing!" Babe shouted gaily, doing a series of spins and jumps. "We were just dancing around down here!"

Lenny looked at the furniture lying on the floor with bafflement as Babe signaled to Barnette to start dancing with her. Barnette made a noble—if vain—attempt to imitate Baryshnikov. Lenny watched his feeble moves with distaste as she wiped some of her cold cream off her face.

"Well, for heaven's sake," she said at last. "You frightened me to death. I thought . . ."

But she didn't get to say what she thought, for at that moment the phone rang out shrill and loud.

Lenny picked it up: "Hello? Yes, this is Lenny Magrath . . ."

Babe stopped dancing and looked at Lenny. Her older sister's face was turning white with fear. And Babe knew that people's faces only turned that ghastly color when they learned that someone they loved was dead or dying.

Nine

Old Grandaddy was in a coma. He lay in a god-awful maze of tubes, a sickening echo of the man who had once taken his granddaughters out to eat banana splits for breakfast. A respirator was all that was keeping him alive—and that just barely. Each grim breath he sucked in appeared to be his last.

Lenny and Babe sat beside his bed watching him in silence. How long they had been at his side, they had no idea. They had arrived at the hospital only a few minutes after Lenny had received the phone call from Old Grandaddy's doctor in which she'd learned that Old Grandaddy had had what appeared to be his last stroke and had lapsed into a coma.

It terrified Lenny to see Old Grandaddy dying. All the other times he had been in the hospital, the doctor had assured her he would recover. This time, the doctor had suggested she find a way to say good-bye to him. Only how could she say good-bye to someone who couldn't hear her?

Lenny shook her head. Trying to picture her life without Old Grandaddy to care for was impossible. People needed a reason to get up in the morning, people needed someone to love. While life with Old Grandaddy hadn't been pleasant, it had at least been bearable. And if the house had seemed peculiarly empty with just the two of them in it, how was it going to feel with just herself?

Babe was less crushed by the prospect of Old Grandaddy's demise. He was very old, after all, and how much fun could it be to keep kicking about on earth after almost all your blood vessels had popped in your brain? Anyhow, it seemed to Babe that with Old Grandaddy out of the way, Lenny might start figuring out a way to begin living *her* life.

Old Grandaddy let loose a kind of rattling sound from his throat. No doubt about it, he was on his way to a place far, far better than this one.

Babe and Lenny looked at each other fearfully. They had taken turns through the night trying to reach Meg by phone, but where she was was anyone's guess. It would be terrible for Old Grandaddy to die without Meg knowing, and yet it seemed as though that was just what was going to happen.

The sun was only beginning to rise. Meg and Doc lay in a clearing of the woods, sound asleep as huge pine trees whistled in the air over them, and birds chirped with joy at the start of a wondrous day.

Meg felt light on her eyes and slowly began to wake. She smelled the pine and heard the river rushing. For a moment she wondered lazily where she was, and then she felt Doc's warm body beside her and she smiled with understanding as she opened her eyes.

The air was full of white mist that gave the trees a dreamy, half-hidden look. Meg stared at them. They seemed to stretch out for miles and miles, so strong and certain and triumphant in their height.

Meg turned toward Doc and softly began singing "Don't Fence Me In" to his still-sleeping face. Doc's eyes opened to Meg's beautiful sounds. The song she was singing not only happened to be his favorite, it also happened to be a happy song. Not sad like all the songs she had once sung. He grinned at her as she continued singing, and then he looked up at the perfect blue sky over his head.

Meg's voice filled the air as she sang louder and stronger. Soon her song was as powerful as the pine trees around her. She had found her voice, had found in her night with Doc a reason to sing again. And she knew—she absolutely knew—that today was going to be the most glorious day of her life. She was going to make amends. Going to apologize to Babe and Lenny. And—this most important of all—she was going to have a talk with Old Grandaddy, going to explain all the lies she had been feeding him.

Oh, yes, everything was going to be absolutely wonderful from now on. . . .

Babe and Lenny dragged their tired bodies out the doors of the hospital where Old Grandaddy still lay in his death-rattling coma. The doctor had told them to go home and get some sleep, that he would call if there were any changes in old Grandaddy's condition.

The sisters shuffled slowly to Lenny's car, their eyes bleak and dark-circled from bone weariness.

Lenny sighed. "Babe, I feel bad. I feel *real* bad."

"Why, Lenny?"

"Because I . . . I wished it."

Babe looked up at her older sister with a puzzled frown. "You wished what?"

"I wished that Old Grandaddy would be put out of his pain. I wished on one of my birthday candles. And now he's in this coma and they say he's feeling no pain."

Babe knew how hard all this was on Lenny. Lenny had cried through many long nights at Old Grandaddy's side. Babe desperately wanted to do or say something that might take away some of Lenny's pain, but what was there to be done? Trying to tell her it was just as well that Old Grandaddy died made no sense. Lenny would just feel hurt about words like that. Babe thought and thought. Poor Lenny, all alone and without love just two days after her miserable, uncelebrated thirtieth birthday.

Suddenly Babe had an idea. "Well, when did you have a cake?" she asked eagerly. "I don't remember you having a cake."

Lenny turned away from her little sister with embarrassment. "Well, I didn't . . . have a cake. But I just blew out the candles anyway."

"Oh. Well, those birthday wishes don't count unless you have a cake."

Lenny, whose thinking was a little foggy after a sleepless night, was intrigued by Babe's explanation. "They don't?"

"No," Babe said confidently. And then, more realistically, "A lot of time they don't even count when you *do* have a cake. It just depends."

"Depends on what?"

Babe considered for a moment as Lenny looked at her anxiously. What was it exactly that made the difference between an ineffectual birthday wish and one that actually could come true? Finally Babe said, "It depends on how deep your wish is, I suppose."

At last the sisters reached Lenny's car and got in. They were both exhausted and looked forward to getting some sleep. Neither of them spoke as Lenny drove carefully back to the house, but as they pulled onto their street and saw who was waiting for them, both of them moaned.

Chick was pacing back and forth in her front yard, eating away at her sixth donut of the morning. She had heard of Old Grandaddy's latest bout at death's doorstep and was eager to find out from Lenny whether he had kicked the bucket yet.

At the sight of Lenny's car, Chick began flailing her arms and running toward the Magrath house. She caught up with the car when Lenny pulled into the drive.

"Lenny! Oh Lenny!"

Lenny sighed and went over to her cousin. Babe lingered at a safe distance.

"Well," Chick began brightly. "Is he still in the coma?"

"Uh-huh."

Chick nodded as she reached into her pocket

for a piece of paper. "Well, it seems to me we'd better get busy phoning." And she unfolded the paper to reveal a list of names. "Now I've made out this list of all the people we need to notify about Old Grandaddy's predicament. I'll phone half if you'll phone half."

Disgusted, Babe walked away from Lenny and Chick and flopped her sleepy body down on the front steps of the house as Lenny took the list from Chick and ripped off half of it.

Chick did not like Lenny's attitude, and was about to remark as to how she did not particularly relish having to even phone half the people on the list when she was, after all, only one-fourth of the granddaughters, but then she recalled that she had left Annie May in her kitchen with breakfast cooking and that she should get home before her house burst into flames or some such thing. So she scrambled off in frustration, not even able to toss in a few gems about Meg's trashy disappearance for the night.

Lenny eyed her list briefly—Uncle Spark Dude, Sally May, and on and on and on—and then walked slowly to the steps where Babe waited for her. Sighing simultaneously, they walked in the house and trudged off to the room they loved best—the kitchen. There, Lenny began making waffles for both of them while Babe stared out the window at the swing dangling from the oak tree.

Always before, Babe had derived some peace from looking at that swing. She had liked the way it always swayed back and forth with such regularity. But now as she peered out at it, the swing looked horribly like a cat dangling from a noose. Babe shuddered and sat down at the table so she wouldn't have to see the swing anymore.

Lenny cracked eggs into a mixing bowl, then glanced at the screen door. "Gosh," she said, "I wonder when Meg's coming home."

"Should be soon," Babe said optimistically. Lord, she did hope Meg hadn't taken it into her head to run off to Canada or some other foreign land with Doc.

Lenny added some flour and milk to the eggs, then poured her batter into an ancient waffle iron. "I guess it hurts my feelings," she said, "the way old Grandaddy's always put so much stock in Meg and all her singing talent. I think I've been, well, envious of her 'cause I can't seem to do too much."

Babe glanced indignantly at Lenny. "Why, sure you can."

"I can?"

"Sure! You just have to put your mind to it; that's all. It's like how I went out and bought the saxophone, just hoping I'd be able to attend music school and start up my own career." Babe sighed at the memory of how much hope she had once had that she could turn herself into a great blues musician, go on tours someday through smoky nightclubs in towns with exotic names such as Harlem. "Of course, now it just doesn't look like things are gonna work out for me. But I know they would for you."

"Well," Lenny began hopefully, "they'll work out for you, too."

Babe eyed her sister skeptically.

"Listen," Lenny continued, "I heard up at the hospital that Zackery's already in fair condition. They say he'll probably be able to walk and everything."

But this news didn't exactly set Babe's spirits soaring. Staring at the table, she whispered, "Yeah. And life sure can be miserable."

Lenny nodded and for a time the sisters sat glum and silent at the table musing over the rottenness of their lives. Then, smelling something burning, Lenny glanced at the waffle iron. Although the thing had always run too hot, she couldn't quite believe the waffles could already be done. And yet, when she hurried over and opened up the iron, the waffles were black and smoking.

Lenny began to cry. Waffles burnt beyond recognition . . . Billy Boy electrocuted . . . Old Grandaddy as good as buried . . . Babe en route to prison . . . and Meg—where in the world was Meg?

Meg happened to be in the front seat of Doc's pickup where she lay merrily piling empty beer cans on her chest as Doc careened recklessly along the streets of Hazlehurst with the kind of confidence only the drunkest of drivers are able to possess. The pickup swayed this way and that until it finally reached the Magrath's street and came to a tremendous, screeching halt in front of Lenny's house.

Chick, hearing not only the sound of the truck but also what seemed to her to be extremely lewd laughter, ran to her kitchen window to see what was going on.

A door of the pickup opened, and Chick watched with bulging eyes as a slew of empty liquor bottles and beer cans tumbled to the ground, followed by what Chick first thought was a dead dog but which gradually appeared to be her cousin Meg. Meg stumbled a few steps before collapsing to the ground and Chick shook her head with happy disgust. Meg's clothes were wrinkled, *barely on*, and quite obviously the same clothes she had worn the night before.

In a moment, Doc lumbered out onto the lawn and tried to lift Meg up without falling over himself. The two laughed wildly as Doc at last managed to get Meg to her feet, then laughed even harder when they realized she was only wearing one shoe.

Meg wandered lopsidedly about searching for her missing high heel in the debris of cans and bottles, at last finding it—broken in half at the heel. She held it triumphantly, then embraced Doc with passion.

Chick smacked her lips as Doc and Meg groped at each other in a manner that Chick could only liken to wild animals in heat.

Finally Doc and Meg parted. He got in his truck and she wandered in zigzags toward the house. Her steps, though awkward and alcoholic, were happy ones. And though she was aware that her cousin was watching her from the house next door with seething eyes, she couldn't have cared less. Even Chick couldn't take away Meg's fantastic, lighthearted mood. Smiling and holding the broken heel of her shoe to her mouth like a microphone, she began singing with the voice of a drunken angel as she bounded up the front porch steps.

"Good morning! Good morning!" she shouted out joyfully as she burst into the living room.

Babe and Lenny, too depressed to do more than look up from their burnt waffles, could hear the sound of bourbon in Meg's happy cry. As for Meg, she cheerfully followed the smell of cooking into the kitchen. There, Lenny and Babe eyed her with gloom, but she didn't notice their long faces, circled eyes, and weary bodies. Instead she laughed radiantly and limped toward them clutching her broken shoe. "Good morning!" she shouted out again, but her sisters remained mute.

Meg looked around her with the ecstasy of obliviousness. "Oh, it's a wonderful morning!" she told Babe and Lenny. "I tell you, I am surprised I feel this good. I should feel like hell. By all accounts, I should feel like utter hell."

Her sisters, who *were* feeling like utter hell, looked down at the kitchen table and thought about ways to tell Meg what had happened to Old Grandaddy in her absence, but before they could even begin with their story, Meg was hobbling about the kitchen and ranting about her shoe. "Where's the glue?" she asked no one in particular. "This damn heel has broken off my shoe."

Round and round the room in circles Meg wandered, singing loudly, until at last she located a bottle of glue. "Ah! Here it is!" she announced.

And then, seeing Lenny and Babe glance up

at her with sorrow: "Well, what's wrong with you two? My God, you look like doom!"

Lenny's lips parted. How could she tactfully tell Meg that while she was off drinking with Doc, Old Grandaddy had crawled into the jaws of death? She looked into Meg's rapture-filled eyes and began to talk, but Meg instantly interrupted.

"Oh I know," Meg said lightly. "You're mad at me 'cause I stayed out all night long. Well . . . I did."

Lenny shook her head wearily. "No. We're . . . we're not mad at you. We're just . . . depressed." And with that said, Lenny found herself starting to sob.

Meg, a little alarmed by how intensely her sister was reacting to her night with Doc, hobbled over to Lenny. "Lenny, listen to me now, everything's all right with Doc. I mean, nothing happened." And then, flashing a grin at Babe, "Well, actually, *a lot* did happen, but it didn't come to anything. Not because of me, I'm afraid."

Lenny looked away from Meg with hopelessness as Meg blithely continued with her tale. "I mean, I was out there thinking, What will I say when he begs me to run away with him? Will I have pity on his wife and those two half-Yankee children? I mean, can I sacrifice their happiness for mine? Yes! Oh yes I can! But . . ." And here Meg tried to show the significance of what she was saying by wagging her glue bottle. "He didn't ask me. He didn't even *want* to ask me."

Now Meg opened her glue bottle and began repairing her heel. "Why aren't I miserable?"

she asked her sisters. "I should be humiliated! Devastated! But I'm happy. I realized I could care about someone. I could want someone. I sang all night long! And none of it was to please Old Grandaddy!"

Nervously Lenny and Babe eyed each other. "Ah, Meg," Babe began.

"What?"

"Well, it's just—it's . . ." But Babe couldn't say it. Meg was in such wildly good spirits, it seemed absolutely criminal to tell her about Old Grandaddy.

So Lenny tried: "It's about Old Grandaddy."

Meg waved her hand impatiently. "Oh, I know. I told him all those stupid lies. Well. I'm gonna go right over there this morning and tell him the truth. And if he can't take it, if it sends him into a coma, well, that's just too damn bad."

Babe's and Lenny's eyes met the moment Meg said the word *coma,* and each sister started to smile. Finally, her smile turning to a sly grin, Babe whispered, "You're too late," and then began to laugh.

Lenny tried to control her own impulse to giggle. "Oh stop," she told Babe—even though she herself was starting to sputter. "Please!"

Meg looked at her laughing sisters with happy curiosity. "What is it? What's so funny?"

"It's not funny," Babe said honestly, desperately trying to get control of herself.

"No, it's not," Lenny agreed, as she too found herself unable to stop laughing. "It's not a *bit* funny."

"Well, what is it then? What?"

Breathing deeply to rid herself of every last hysterical giggle, Babe said, "Well, it's just—it's just—"

"What?"

"Well, Old Grandaddy . . . he . . . he . . ." And here Babe could no longer control herself. Erupting with wild laughter that could just as well have been wild sobbing, Babe shouted, "He's in a coma!"

Shocked, Meg stared at Babe. "He's *what*?"

"In a *coma*!" Babe shrieked.

Meg stood aghast as Lenny and Babe slid down in their chairs with breathless giggles. "My God," she told both of them. "That's not funny."

Managing to calm down a bit, Babe earnestly agreed. "I know. I know. For some reason it just struck us as . . . funny."

Lenny, wiping tears of laughter from her face, tried to explain. "I'm sorry. It's . . . it's not funny. It's *very* sad. We've been up all night long."

"We're *really* tired," Babe added.

"Well, my God," Meg whispered. "How is he? Is he gonna live?"

Once more Babe and Lenny made the fatal mistake of looking at each other. Again they broke up with uproarious, unwanted laughter. "They don't think so!" Babe at last managed to say.

Meg turned from Babe to Lenny with alarm. She couldn't understand how her sisters could yuck it up over Old Grandaddy's coma.

Lenny saw the outrage in Meg's eyes and tried to collect herself. "Oh I don't know why we're like this," she said between chuckles. "We're just sick. We're just awful!"

Babe nodded solemnly. "We are. We're just awful."

Lenny looked down at the table and willed herself to think about her shrunken ovary. "Oh good," she said in a moment. "Now I feel bad. Now I feel like crying. I do, I feel like crying."

Babe, who was herself trying to stop laughing by picturing a lifetime in prison without either Willie Jay *or* Barnette to comfort her during the endless nights, nodded. "Me too. Me too."

Meg shook her head. Here she had just gone and found some joy in life, and she had to get all this rotten news. "Well, you've gotten *me* depressed."

"I'm sorry," Lenny said sympathetically. "It, ah, happened last night. He had another"—and suddenly Lenny was off again with gales of laughter—"another *stroke*!"

"I see," Meg said quietly as Babe joined Lenny once more in reckless, abandoned mirth at the horror of not only Old Grandaddy's fate, but their own as well.

"But he's stabilized now," Lenny added, her words barely decipherable through her screams and giggles.

Meg looked at her sleep-starved, hysterical sisters. Both of them were laughing so hard they were clutching their sides. She grimaced. How typical of Old Grandaddy to go and do something that would prevent her from being able to feel good about herself. Here she was going to come clean about all her lying and he had to hurl himself into a stupid coma. It just didn't seem fair.

Meg set down her glued high heel and sighed. So Old Grandaddy was dying and her sisters were losing their minds. Life sure had a way of bursting bubbles. . . .

At noon Lenny woke to the sounds of "I've Been Working on the Railroad" coming from down the hall in Old Grandaddy's room. At first she thought it was Old Grandaddy himself banging away on the piano, but then as she sat up and rubbed the sleep from her eyes she realized it had to be Meg. Old Grandaddy had taught her that song when she was just a little girl. Lenny had been jealous watching Meg sitting on his lap, her little fingers making Old Grandaddy beam with pride as they precociously found the right keys. But now Lenny didn't feel jealous at all for some reason. She was happy Meg could play the piano—happy that at least somebody in the family could do something other than sit and cry.

Lenny hurried to join Meg. Her sister smiled up at her briefly as she came into the room, then went back to her playing. Lenny looked around the room at all of Old Grandaddy's treasures. He was—had been—a Civil War buff. The room was full of history books, yellowed maps of the once-great Confederacy, antique rifles, and framed charts. There were also endless family photos, some dating back to the last century. After Old Grandaddy had gotten so sick he'd had to take to his bed, Lenny had brought his dinner up to him and would sit on a chair and listen as he told her stories about the family. His eyes had shone when he'd talked about his days of courting Old Grandmama. "I know it's hard for you to believe it," he'd say, "but she was the most popular gal in all of Copiah County in her day. Lordy, I almost choked when she said she'd taken a fancy to me. I was that in love, I was."

Now Lenny looked at a photograph of Old Grandaddy in his wedding tuxedo. He'd been a handsome man—dancing eyes like Meg's, and talented like her, too. He'd been able to sing, play musical instruments, do card tricks, wiggle his ears, you name it.

Feeling her eyes start to fill with tears, Lenny turned away from the picture and walked over to Old Grandaddy's fish tank. The water in it needed changing desperately. Pathetic fish swam about in gray-green water that smelled even worse than it looked. Lenny figured she should change the water, but she just didn't feel the strength. Instead she gave the fish some food, which they instantly lapped up like the little slum dwellers they had become since Old Grand-daddy had left them in Lenny's care. She watched the fish gobble flakes of food, then gently spit them out seconds later. That's how the water gets so dirty, Lenny thought. They spit as much food out as they eat.

"Things sure are gonna be different around here when Old Grandaddy dies," Lenny said at last.

Meg stopped playing the piano and glanced at Lenny.

"Well, not for you two really," Lenny added, "but for me."

Meg shook her head. While Lenny and Babe had been napping away their hysterics, she'd been trying to sort things out in her head about Lenny and Old Grandaddy and what Lenny should do now that he was finally dying. "Oh, come on now, Lenny, you're your own woman. Invite some people over. Have some parties. Go out with strange men."

"I don't know any strange men."

"Well," Meg said quietly, "you know that Charlie."

Lenny sighed. Just thinking about Charlie made her feel like throwing herself out a window. "I told him we should never see each other again."

Meg looked at Lenny aghast. *Lenny* had broken up with *Charlie*? So there *had* been more to the story than what Babe had known. Lenny, the martyr that she was, had probably thought she had a duty to break up with the guy on account of her ovary problem. "Well," Meg said at last, "if you told him, you can just untell him."

"Oh, no," Lenny insisted. "I couldn't. I'd be too scared." And with that said, Lenny left the room so Meg couldn't push her on the subject.

Babe had come from the downstairs porch, where she had been napping, and was sitting, still yawning and listless, on the window seat in the hallway. Lenny looked at her a moment, then started to head down the stairway. But before she had even gotten two steps down, Meg was coming after her.

Lenny hurried toward the landing, but Meg called out after her, "What harm could it possibly do? I mean, it's not gonna make things any worse than this never seeing him again, at all, forever."

Lenny stopped, and looked up at Meg. She was about to shout that Meg's suggestion was utterly ridiculous, but suddenly she realized that Meg had a point—an extremely good point. Just how could her life possibly get worse? Even if Charlie said hearing her voice made him want to vomit, could that *truly* make her life worse? What could be bleaker than not even having the hope of ever seeing Charlie again? So, a little nervously, Lenny said, "I suppose that's true."

Delighted, Meg pressed on. "Of course it is. So call him up! Take a chance, will you?"

Lenny looked at Meg anxiously. She had never taken a chance in her life; wasn't it a bit late to start now?

Babe ran over to the top of the stairs and joined Meg in urging Lenny. "You've got to try, Lenny. I think you do."

"Really?" Lenny asked, almost hopeful now. "Really? *Really?*"

Both her sisters nodded vigorously. "Yes!" Meg shouted.

Babe gave Lenny an imploring gaze. "You should."

Like a fearful athlete about to take his first steps onto the playing field, Lenny began giving herself a private pep talk. All she had to do was dial Charlie's number, tell him she'd been wrong to break off with him. It wasn't like she had to look at him while she said those things. It would almost be like saying them just to a mirror or something. And suppose Charlie was happy to hear from her? Just suppose he was as miserable as she was at being alone? Suppose he actually wanted to see her again?

Lenny looked at her sisters. Their faces were so eager, so positive, so convinced that she had a chance for love. "All right!" she shouted. "I will! I will!" And she tore down the steps to the telephone in the kitchen.

For a time, Meg and Babe waited at the top of the steps and listened for the sound of Lenny's voice on the phone. But when no sound came, they decided maybe their presence was making Lenny nervous and went outside. Meg sat down on the rope swing that dangled from the old oak and lit a cigarette while Babe walked through the garden.

It seemed to Meg that Babe was troubled about something that went deeper than everything with Old Grandaddy and Zackery. It wasn't like Babe to just walk off by herself, not to want to sit by Meg. Meg watched her little sister. Babe was wringing her hands as she strolled past the pawpaws in the yard.

Meg was just about ready to go over to Babe and ask her what was weighing on her so hard when Babe ran back into the house. Meg shrugged. Maybe there wasn't anything really bothering Babe so much. Maybe she was just all concerned about whether Lenny had called Charlie or not. So Meg let her thoughts drift away from her little sister and over to her night with Doc as she swung higher and higher in the air. Closing her eyes, she let herself fly. It was important not to let go of the joy she had found in the night, important not to forget that she was alive, that her life could go forward even if Old Grandaddy's was coming to an end.

Back and forth Meg went, her heart trying to keep hold of the songs she had just started to want to sing again. She didn't notice Babe coming back out of the house, didn't open her eyes to see her little sister climbing the old oak tree with the envelope of photographs Barnette had given her just before Lenny had gotten the phone call from the hospital.

Babe crawled up to the very highest branches of the tree and clutched the photographs to her chest. Meg looked so happy swinging down below her. Meg had found love. And Lenny, off in the kitchen still trying to work up the courage to dial her Charlie's number—Lenny, too, was in pursuit of love. Both her sisters were going to be fine, she thought. Their lives were going to unfold in a vivid, new way, because they had found a way to touch their lives against other people's lives. But Babe didn't see how her life could ever link up with another person's again. What had she brought to Willie Jay by touching his life other than kicks in the head? And what was she going to give to Barnette other than a losing case?

Meg stopped pumping her legs and began to coast on her swing. Babe waited until Meg had opened her eyes again and then she called down to her sister, "Meg?"

Meg looked up, startled to hear a voice from the sky. Then she saw Babe staring at her and she smiled. "What?"

But Babe didn't quite know how to begin. She needed to tell someone about the photographs, and yet she was embarrassed. "Nothing."

Meg frowned. "You okay?"

Babe sighed and slid down the trunk of the tree. When she got to the ground, she eyed Meg for a moment, then handed her the envelope. If there was someone in the family who could understand wild, passionate sex scenes, it was Meg. "Here," she said. "Take a look. It's some evidence Zackery's collected against me. Looks like my goose is cooked."

Holding one of the photographs up to the light of the day, Meg stared with wide eyes. The picture was blurry, but it clearly showed Babe, naked, standing beside an exceptionally well-built black man. "My God, it's you and . . . is that Willie Jay?"

Babe nodded.

"Well, he certainly *has* grown. You were right about that. My oh my."

Flipping through the pictures, Meg felt her heart racing with a feeling of doom. There were photographs of Willie Jay and Babe making love in every possible position, and even a few positions that seemed to Meg to be quite impossible: Willie Jay and Babe on top of a car, under a car, inside a car; Willie Jay and Babe in a wheelbarrow, a golf cart, and upon a bicycle built for two. . . . And in every picture, Dog stood patiently watching, his head cocked curiously to one side.

"Please don't tell Lenny," Babe whispered. "She'd hate me."

"I won't," Meg assured her, knowing Lenny

would not so much feel hate as she would feel utter disbelief. "I won't tell."

After going through all the photographs—very thoroughly—Meg slid them back in their envelope and returned them to Babe, who leaned against the oak tree lifeless with gloom.

"What are you going to do?" Meg asked.

Babe stared sadly at the rope on the swing. "What *can* I do?"

Ten

Zackery Botrelle lay in his hospital bed heaving and sighing like a beached whale as Barnette stood at his side politely explaining that he intended to expose Zackery to all of Hazlehurst as the wife beater he was.

Three of Zackery's legal associates were in the room with Barnette and Zackery, and their eyebrows were raised with the fear of public exposure. But Zackery himself was nonplussed. It wasn't in his nature to take seriously the complaints of anyone smaller or poorer than he was. All his life he had seen that the average person could be intimidated by wealth and physical bulk. And he didn't see any reason to think that the slender young man before him was going to be an exception to his rule that if the human soul couldn't be bought, it could at least be stamped into ruin.

Barnette handed Zackery the photostatic copies of Babe's medical reports. Zackery flipped through the documents with boredom. Finally he slammed them across his bed and snorted. "Those half-assed medical reports won't hold up in court," he told Barnette. "They don't prove anything except that I have a very clumsy wife."

It took every ounce of self-control Barnette could muster up in himself to keep from grabbing Zackery's smug, snide face and bashing it against the bars of the bed. How Babe could have endured living with such a man was beyond Barnette's comprehension. Why his sweet buttercup hadn't gotten murderous notions on her mind the moment she said the words "I do" was baffling. What a sweet lamb she was to have taken so long before aiming a gun at this monster's corrupt heart!

Keeping his hands at his sides, Barnette spoke to Zackery with a tight, cool voice: "I also have some eyewitnesses. And they're not only willing to testify; they're anxious."

For a moment Zackery looked a bit ruffled. His mind flashed to the hundreds of people he had wronged since childhood—playmates whose kittens he had dropped down sewers; girls in high school whose reputations he had ruined because they had refused him a date; college classmates whose cars he had deliberately smashed into when they scored higher than he had on a test; clients whose money he had carelessly squandered; neighbors whose gestures of kindness he had taken pleasure in snubbing. There wasn't a person in Hazlehurst he hadn't hurt, with the exception of his dear, dead mummy, whom he hadn't been able to hurt because she had been ever fatter and richer and meaner than he. But for all that Zackery knew the townspeople had a grudge against him, he couldn't see why they would cause him any trouble. "Everyone has their price," he told Barnette. "Besides, the real dynamite is in the vacation photos I've got of my sugar wife and her yard boy."

Barnette smiled. "Actually, Senator Botrelle, I don't think those photos are going to flatter you at all. Folks around here may start to question certain aspects of your *leadership* qualities."

Suddenly Zackery began to feel genuine fear. As an elected official, he depended on a certain kind of image and that could not be the image of a man whose wife had given him horns. He glanced quickly at his aides for a response. They, fearful of Zackery's wrath, looked about the room as though they hadn't heard a thing, but Zackery knew that their absence of opinion was a confirmation of what Barnette was saying.

Zackery gave Barnette a keen glance, saw for the first time that the peculiar boy he was dealing with was shrewder than he'd given him credit for being. "Tell me," he said at last, "just what sort of settlement did you have in mind?"

"I don't want her serving any time."

Zackery sneered. "What? In jail? No, I don't think we have to send her to jail. The public wouldn't like seeing pretty little Babe sent off to the slammer."

Barnette stared at Zackery with his intense, razor eyes. He knew Zackery had some card up his sleeve. "Then you'll drop all charges?"

But Zackery only grinned. "I'll tell you what. I'm gonna seriously consider doing just that. But first you better do something about that nigger kid of hers. Or he could end up screwed, chewed, and bar-be-qued." And with that Zackery began to chortle with delight at his talent for rhyming.

Barnette said nothing, but his fear that Zackery had a clearly marked plan for retaliation against Babe continued. But what could the plan be? If Zackery wasn't going to press charges, what could he possibly do to Babe? Have her gunned down by one of his advisers? Unlikely. And yet Zackery seemed so certain that he hadn't lost yet. . . .

After collecting his documents, Barnette quietly left Zackery's hospital room and drove over to the tiny, tar-papered house where Willie Jay lived with his mother Cora and his many brothers and sisters. As gently as possible, Barnette explained to the boy that he would have to leave town that very afternoon or risk being hung in the night by certain members of a club known for wearing white sheets when it wasn't Halloween.

Willie Jay, a gentle boy with large, velvet eyes, nodded solemnly and packed up his few possessions while his mother stood in the background crying. Barnette assured Cora that he would make certain her son had enough money to get started up north, and then he and Willie Jay left.

Barnette's heart broke when they reached his car and a large, friendly dog came trotting over to them. So this was the famous Dog, who had brought Babe and Willie Jay together in the first place.

Willie Jay looked up at Barnette with imploring eyes as he knelt petting Dog and saying his farewell. For a time Barnette stood hopelessly by, thinking it was utter folly for Willie Jay to bring the animal with him, but at last he told the boy to bring Dog along. And then the three were off—first to Barnette's house to get a disguise for Willie Jay to wear in case any of Zackery's pals were already hanging out at the bus station, and then over to the Magraths' house.

Babe was inconsolable about Willie Jay's having to leave. She felt it was all her fault that her friend had to go away from his home and family. Barnette explained to her that at least he would have Dog with him, but this didn't seem to bring much comfort to her.

Barnette, Willie Jay, Dog, Babe, and Meg rode to the bus station in somber silence. Willie Jay played with his disguise so that by the time he got out of the car he was wearing a pair of sunglasses, a sombrero, and a poncho.

Meg and Barnette stood at a discreet distance as Babe said her good-byes to Willie Jay and Dog. Her eyes filled with tears, as did Willie Jay's . . . as did Dog's. Then Willie Jay ambled onto the bus with his faithful friend. The last thing Babe saw, he and Dog had their faces pressed to the window. Willie Jay's sunglasses looked overwhelmingly strange and large on his youthful, innocent face. Dog's sunglasses looked even more peculiar.

Babe waved a sad hand as the bus rolled into the distance, then began to sob woefully when she heard Dog barking out a farewell to her.

Barnette and Meg went over to her and led her slowly back to Barnette's car. The three drove along in depressed silence. Barnette ached to see how much his angel had loved Willie Jay . . . and Dog. Meg felt awful with the thought that Babe still wasn't safe as long as Zackery had those trashy pictures of her, and Babe was heartbroken to have destroyed Willie Jay's life.

Meg lit a cigarette and propped her feet up on the dashboard. Babe stared out the car window, watching blankly as Barnette drove past streets full of people staring and pointing at the sad-eyed girl.

At last Barnette spoke. "I'm sorry, Becky. It seemed the only way."

Babe was too full of despair to do more than nod. And when Barnette's car pulled up to the Magrath house, she still couldn't find any words for him. It seemed to her that all she could bring to Barnette would be the same ruination she had brought to Willie Jay. Already she was certain Barnette was going to lose his very first law case all on account of her. And so, when she climbed out of his car, her only words to him were "Good-bye, Barnette." And he, feeling he had destroyed her life by sending away Willie Jay, was only able to respond, "Good-bye, Becky."

Lenny stood in the bedroom staring into the mirror over her bureau. All afternoon she had been struggling unsuccessfully to dial Charlie's phone number in Memphis. Sometimes she had made it all the way up to the last digit, but always she had ended up flinging down the telephone in terror. Her mouth would go dry; her heart would start to explode; her mind would reel with embarrassing thoughts. What if he didn't remember her? What if he told her the thought of a woman with a deformed ovary was repugnant to him?

She picked up a bottle of perfume and sprayed it all over her body in a vague effort to make herself smell as sexy as she imagined women with two working ovaries smelled. Then, for what seemed the thousandth time that afternoon, she went over to the phone and picked up the receiver. But the perfume didn't help her any. Once again, she hung up the phone. And then, with self-loathing, she made a face at herself in the mirror. Weak, chicken hearted, mousy thing, she told her face. You miserable, wretched spinster.

With absolute frustration, she tore out of the room and raced down the steps to the living room where Babe sat on a window seat sucking at a lemon.

Babe didn't even hear Lenny coming toward her. Lost in her own despair, she rocked back and forth with futile thoughts of Willie Jay and Barnette. Over and over, she whispered, "Good-bye Barnette . . . Good-bye Becky," and then, "Good-bye Willie Jay . . . Good-bye Becky."

Lenny raced up to Babe in a fluster. "Oh! Oh! Oh! I'm so ashamed! I'm such a coward! I just couldn't make the call! My heart was pounding like a hammer. Why, I could actually see my blouse moving back and forth!"

Still lost in her own misery, Babe scarcely looked up to see Lenny demonstrating the movements her blouse had taken.

Lenny took her little sister's depression as a sign that Babe was as disgusted with her as she was herself. "Oh, Babe, you look so disappointed. Are you?"

"Uh-huh," Babe whispered lifelessly.

"Oh no!" Lenny cried. "I can't stand it! I've gone and disappointed my little sister, Babe! Oh *no*! I feel like howling like a dog!"

But before she could actually do such a thing, someone else did it for her: "Oooooh, Lenny!" came a screeching call from outside, and in a moment Chick was banging open the living-room door with high drama and a great show of sympathy. Ignoring Lenny's obvious stress and Babe's obvious sorrow, she oozed her way to the center of the room as she wrung her hands and made cooing sounds. "Well, I just don't know what to say," she began, her voice taking on the tones of a doctor's when he is telling the patient that she has only a day to live. "I am *so* sorry for you! I mean, to have such a sister as *that*!"

Glancing uncertainly at Babe, Lenny said, "What do you mean?"

Chick smiled with condescension. "Oh, you don't need to pretend with me. I saw Meg stumbling out of Doc Porter's pickup truck and her looking such a *disgusting* mess."

Lenny's jaw dropped open as Chick walked toward her drenched in sympathy. "You must be *so* ashamed. Why, I always said that girl was nothing but cheap Christmas trash."

"Don't talk that way about Meg," Lenny said quietly.

Chick laughed. "Oh come on now, Lenny honey. Why, Meg's a low-class tramp and you need not have one more blessed thing to do with her and her disgusting behavior."

For a moment, Lenny started to hang her head in the shameful manner she had hung it her whole life. But then the force of Chick's words hit her. To stand like a puppy while Chick insulted Meg, called her sister a cheap tramp, was not only cowardly, it was a terrible injustice against Meg. Meg was not only her sister; Meg was a good and kind human being as well. For years and years Lenny had let Chick put her down, make remarks about Meg and Babe and Lenny herself. And Lenny had let it all happen because her embarrassment about her family had always been stronger than her loyalty to them. But now, in the cruelty of Chick's words, she found the love she had for her sister begin to soar over her fear and embarrassment. So she raised her head high, straightened her back, and slowly spoke: "I said, don't you ever talk that way about my sister Meg again."

Chick gave Lenny a look of shock. "Well, goodness gracious, Lenora, don't be such a noodle. It's the truth!"

Lenny's back was now ramrod straight and her eyes were dancing with fury. "I don't care if it's the Ten Commandments," she told her cousin, "I don't want to hear it in my home. Not ever again."

Chick hurled a hand to her heart and stared at Lenny in disbelief. "In *your* home?" And looking around the living room with the air of one soon to take possession: "Why, this is *my* grandfather's home! And you're just living here on his charity, so don't you get high-falutin' with me, Miss Lenora Josephine Magrath!"

But Lenny's eyes were burning hotter than

her cousin's inflammatory words. All her life she had acted like a charity case, all her life she had been showing gratitude to people who made her feel that they were being gracious just for letting her breathe. But no more. "Get out of here," she told Chick.

Now Chick's jaw dropped open. She couldn't believe Lenny was talking to her this way. Lenny, the frumpiest mouse on the planet, trying to boss a member of the Ladies' Social League! "Don't you tell me to get out!" she bellowed. "Why, I've had just about my fill of you trashy Magraths and your trashy ways: hanging yourselves in cellars, carryin' on with married men"—and turning to Babe with vengeance—"shooting your husbands!"

"Get out!"

Chick ignored Lenny and thrust a finger in Babe's face. Eyes bulging with disgust, she screamed, "And don't think she's not gonna get up at the state prison farm or in some *mental* institution. Why it's a clear-cut case of manslaughter with intent to *kill*!"

Babe's eyes filled with horror and she felt her spine shiver. She hadn't thought of going to a mental hospital—hadn't at all considered the possibility that what she had done to Zackery might add up to her being insane. Somehow the notion of herself as a crazy person was much more frightening to her than thinking of herself as a criminal-type person. Babe cringed before Chick.

As for Lenny, she went wild at the sight of her little sister huddled in a ball with Chick looming over her. Instantly, she advanced on

Chick with a hell-bent fury that scared even the formidable Chick. "Out!" Lenny yelled. "Get *out*!"

Chick began to back her way out of the living room and into the kitchen. "That's what everyone's saying," she screamed, though in her scream there was some terror at the anger in Lenny's eyes. Desperately trying to ignore those eyes, she concentrated on Babe as Lenny continued to pursue her: "*Deliberate* intent to kill! And you'll pay for that! Do you hear me?"

Babe hurled her hands to her ears as Lenny backed Chick into a corner of the kitchen and picked up a broom. Chick was still screaming at Babe and didn't notice the broom in Lenny's hands. "You'll pay!" she kept squealing to the frightened Babe.

Lenny lifted the broom to Chick's face. "And I'm telling you to get out!" she shouted.

For a moment Chick eyed the broom with holy terror. But then her deep-rooted belief in her ability to control her cousin came back to her. "You put that down this minute," she ordered Lenny. "Are you a raving lunatic?"

Lenny slammed the broom down on Chick's ridiculously teased hair and knocked it against her thick skull. "I said for you to get out!"

Chick screamed and began running around the kitchen. "Oh! Oh!" she shrieked as Lenny chased her.

Again the broom came at Chick, this time managing to strike at her oversized target of a rear end. "That means out!" And taking another whump: "And never, never, *never* come back!"

Chick scurried to the kitchen door with Lenny and the broom in hot pursuit. "You're crazy!" she screamed, but her feet moved fast and soon she was bustling down the steps of the porch.

Swinging the broom every which way, Lenny continued after her cousin out into the yard: "Do you hear me, Chick-the-Stick? This is *my* home! This is *my* house!"

Babe came running into the kitchen as the sounds of Chick's shouts got so loud she could hear them even through her plugged-up ears. Dumbstruck, she stood at the kitchen window and watched as Lenny and Chick ran around the yard.

Her eyes gleaming, Lenny took a swat at Chick that sent her cousin racing up the mimosa tree. "Police!" Chick screeched, as though a monster from outer space were after her with an atom bomb. "Police! Police!" And clinging to the branches of the tree as Lenny continued to whack at her: "Help! Help!"

Babe grabbed a handful of popcorn left over from the night before and flung it into the air with joy. She had never, ever seen Lenny stand up to anyone, and to see her actually triumphing over their nasty, hateful cousin made Babe's heart soar. "Yeehah!" she shouted out happily. "Yeehah!"

Suddenly the phone began to ring. Laughing happily, oblivious for the moment to all her sorrows, Babe ran to it: "Hello?"

It was Zackery. He was sitting in his hospital bed wearing a flame-red kimono. Scattered across his sheets were the illicit pictures of Babe and Willie Jay. "Hey there, you little idiot," he cooed into his phone.

Babe stared at her receiver. "Hello, Zackery," she whispered.

"Your moron lawyer show you your pinup pictures?" Zackery asked.

Trying her best to steel herself, Babe gripped her phone tightly. "Yes, he showed them to me."

"Yeah, well, I got an extra set of 'em here. Maybe I'll send 'em on to you so's you can hang 'em on your walls when you move into Whitfield."

Babe's hands began to tremble. "What do you mean? You can't put me out to Whitfield Asylum."

Zackery laughed. He knew Babe had grown up hearing talk about her mother's insanity and that she was terrified of ever going crazy herself. "No one will ever doubt that you're a crazy lunatic," he assured her, " 'cause the whole town knows your mother was as crazy as they come."

Babe burst into furious tears. "Don't you call my mama crazy."

Zackery was pleased with himself. He had aimed for Babe's jugular and he had hit it. She was absolutely terrified to think she might be the child of an insane woman who got her jollies out of strangling cats. "I'm sending you to Whitfield," Zackery whispered to her in a singsong.

"No you're not!" Babe screamed, her eyes wide with fear at thoughts of straitjackets, bars, and electroshock treatments. "You're not gonna! You're *not*!"

She slammed the phone down and stared

wildly ahead of her. Outside the window she could see the tire swing swaying back and forth in the breeze. Her eyes fastened on the thick, nooselike rope. "He's not," she told herself. "He's *not*." And suddenly, thinking only that she couldn't live out her life in an asylum, that she would rather be dead than live like that, she ran toward a cabinet and hurled open a drawer full of string and ribbons. Her heart pounding, her hands shaking and sweating, she looked for a rope as strong as the one Old Grandaddy had used to make the tire swing . . . a rope as thick and sturdy as the one Mama had used on herself and the poor cat. At last she found a red cord several feet long. Desperately she grabbed at it and started to yank it from the drawer when she realized with horror what she was actually planning on doing with the cord. She leaped back from the cord with shock and slammed the drawer shut.

In the distance Babe heard Lenny's footsteps and laughter. Wiping sweat from her face, she moved toward the sound of her sister and looked up to see Lenny coming toward her happily swinging the broom.

"Oh, I feel good!" Lenny called out, her eyes shining with the thrill of her triumph over not only Chick, but herself. "I do! I feel *good*!"

"Good!" Babe called back nervously.

Lenny ran into the kitchen with pure delight, grabbed her little sister, and began dancing in circles with her. As Babe spun round and round, her eyes grew more and more wild. I've got to do it, she thought to herself. I've just got to! As for Lenny, she was so pleased to have finally stood up to the world that she didn't notice anything unusual in her sister. She didn't feel the sweat creeping down Babe's back, didn't see that the smile on Babe's face was a strange, possessed one. All she was aware of was that she had held her head high for the first time since Mama's death. Her spirits were soaring. She felt she could do anything—climb a mountain, dive into the deepest river, why . . . she could even call Charlie!

With a pleased laugh, Lenny stopped dancing. "You know what? I'm gonna call Charlie. I'm gonna call him up right now!"

Her eyes blazing with her own plans, Babe said, "You are?"

"Yeah. I feel like I can really do it!"

Wishing that she felt as though she could really do what she wanted to, Babe said, "You do?"

Lenny nodded with pride. "My courage is up; my heart's in it. No more beating around the bush! Let's strike while the iron is hot!"

To Babe, Lenny's call to action was just the pep talk she needed in order to find the courage to kill herself. Excited by Lenny's noble talk, she ran back to the ribbon drawer as her sister hurried down the hall to the library to call Charlie.

"I'm calling him up, Babe," Lenny shouted over her shoulder. "I'm really gonna do it!"

Babe yanked out her thick red cord again. Tugging at it to test its strength, she called back: "Good! Do it! Good!" And then, with her cord dangling after her, Babe tore up the stairs for her bedroom so she too could "strike while the iron's hot."

Lenny hurried into the library and confidently began dialing Charlie's number. Her shoulders held high, she listened to two rings and then heard Charlie's sweet, drawling voice.

"Hello," he said.

"Hello, Charlie. This is Lenny Magrath."

For a moment there was no sound from the other end of the wire and Lenny began to lose her newfound confidence. Was Charlie going to hang up on her? Was he angry that she had called? But then his voice came out over the line with a sound of happiness and surprise. He asked her how she was doing.

Lenny allowed that she was doing fine, just fine. Another silence followed, as neither she nor Charlie could think of what to say next. But at last, with a crack in her voice, Lenny whispered, "I was, ah, just calling to see how you're getting on."

Charlie said he was getting along okay.

"Well, good," Lenny told him. *"Good."*

And then came the moment Lenny had been dreading. Charlie, his voice cracking with nerves as frayed as her own, said how he had thought she hadn't ever wanted to talk to him again.

Lenny breathed deeply and nodded. "Yes, I know I said that." And playing with the cord on the phone, "Well, the reason I said that before, about not seeing each other again, was 'cause of me, not you."

"What about you?" Charlie asked.

Lenny closed her eyes for strength. "Well, it's just that I . . . I can't have any children. I have this ovary problem." And then she opened her eyes and waited for Charlie to tell her that he was only interested in dating women who could give him a house full of babies.

But what Charlie had to say about babies was quite to the contrary of what Lenny had expected. "I've never seen what all the fuss about babies is about," he told her. "They're just a bunch of wrinkled-up little snot-nosed pigs."

Lenny reeled with laughter. "Why Charlie, what a thing to say! They're not *all* snot-nosed pigs!"

Charlie said they were too.

Now Lenny laughed loud and long. "You think they are? Oh Charlie, stop, stop! You're making me laugh." But Charlie didn't stop. He had a whole list of funny things to say about babies and their diapers, babies and their midnight feedings, babies and their horrible temper tantrums. Lenny clutched her side and continued to giggle until at last Charlie finished with his teasing and told her how silly she had been to throw him out of her life on account of her ovary problems.

"Yes, I guess I was," Lenny said merrily. "I can see now that I was."

"I'm lookin' forward to seeing you," Charlie said shyly.

"You are?"

"Uh-huh. Just tell me when's good for you."

Lenny glanced around the room. "Well, I don't know when, Charlie. Soon." And then, throwing all caution to the wind, "How about, well, how about tonight?" Tonight was just fine with Charlie. He'd get in his car right away and start driving as fast as he could for Hazlehurst. Lenny was thrilled. Charlie had a whole evening planned for the two of them—some dinner at a restaurant they both liked right outside town, and then maybe they could take a stroll in the moonlight and wind up the evening snacking on some of the pawpaws Lenny grew out in her garden. All he wanted to know was if his plan sounded okay to Lenny.

"Well, yes," she said excitedly. "Of course we can do that. Why, they're just ripe for picking up."

"So I'll be gettin' in my car now," Charlie told her.

"All right then. I'll be right here."

"Bye bye, Lenny. Gosh, I'm awfully glad you called."

Lenny said her farewells and then hung up the phone with triumph. Running back to the kitchen, she called out to her little sister: "Babe! Oh Babe! He's coming!" But the kitchen was empty, and so Lenny ran over to the stairs. "Babe?" she called up. "Oh, Babe, where are you?"

Where Babe was happened to be on top of her dresser bureau securing one end of her cord to a heavy light fixture high over her head. She didn't hear her sister shouting for her, so driven was she to get her noose shaped and readied.

Downstairs, Lenny hurried out the back door, thinking maybe her sisters had gone outside. "Babe? Meg?"

No answer.

Lenny felt the late afternoon sun on her face. Deciding to forget about her sisters for now, she smiled and picked up a gardening basket. She could get the pawpaws now and be all ready for Charlie when he came for her. She looked up at the violet blue sky and gazed at the trees swaying high over her head. The world seemed to shimmer before her in a way it hadn't before. "Yes," she whispered to herself, "those pawpaws are just right for picking up." And then, in love with Charlie, with the sunshine, with the feeling of the wind pressing against the clothes on her body, she glided toward the garden, her face glowing with newfound life.

If she had turned and looked to the window of her bedroom, she might have seen her little sister rocking back and forth on the bureau top, the red cord now tightly knotted both to her neck and the light fixture. She might have had time to scream out to Babe and stop her sister from plunging to her death.

But as it was, Lenny didn't look, didn't see anything but the glory of the day, and when a loud, horrible bang broke the silence of the late afternoon, Lenny was already in the garden, too far from the house to take in the sound of her sister's suicide.

Eleven

The citizens of Hazlehurst were indignant. The sheriff had let word drift from his office an hour before that Zackery Botrelle was dropping all legal charges against his wife Babe, and the news had blazed through town like wildfire. So there would be no exciting court trial to attend in Sunday-best clothes, no juicy disclosures of motives for the shooting, no scandalous skeletons dragged before the public eye. Just as sixteen years before, when the townspeople had been deprived of learning the motive behind Mary Magrath's strange killing of her cat, they were to be deprived of learning the motive behind her daughter's equally strange attempted killing of Zackery. Somehow it just didn't seem fair—as though someone had pulled the plug on their TV sets at the climax of their favorite soap opera.

The last rays of the late afternoon sun were sending huge, towering shadows across the white wood porches of Hazlehurst. Women sitting on wicker chairs slicing home-grown vegetables for their family's evening meal, shouted back and forth across their yards: *"You hear how Babe's gone and gotten herself off the hook?" "Yep.*

Looks like the only folks ever gonna learn why she tried to blow off that fat Zack are her sisters. And don't you know they ain't gonna tell anybody—just like they ain't never told nobody why their mama went and hung her old kitty cat on the clothes wire."

Of course what the good people of Hazlehurst didn't realize was that the reason why Lenny, Meg, and Babe hadn't ever told anyone why their mother had killed the cat was because they didn't know why . . . at least not yet.

Babe lay on the floor of her bedroom, her back and head covered with huge pieces of plaster from the ceiling and the broken remnants of the light fixture from which she had tried unsuccessfully to hang herself. Her whole body ached, not only from the force with which she had crashed to the floor when the light fixture had broken, but also from the blow she had received when the fixture had landed on her head. Why, she wondered, did death have to be so damn painful?

Still determined to die, Babe picked herself up from the floor and tried to strangle herself by pulling tightly to the noose on her neck. But her natural instincts for self-preservation wouldn't let her get further than a few coughs and at last she decided to go down to the kitchen and cut the noose free from her neck.

She was running down the stairs, the light fixture banging along behind her, when the telephone began to ring. Its sound irritated Babe. Never before in her life had she let a phone jangle without going to answer it, and she hated having to listen to its incessant cry as she tried to think up another way to do away with herself. Hurrying into the kitchen, she glared at the phone with fury. "Will you shut up!" she screamed, but the phone continued to ring even as Babe searched the kitchen for a knife, so that by the time she finally found the knife and managed to cut the cord from her neck, she was wild with anger at the telephone and ran toward it with her knife raised, determined to stab it to smithereens if it didn't quiet itself down immediately. And sure enough, the second she held the knife over the phone, it went silent. "Thank God," she muttered angrily, and returned to making plans for her next attempt at suicide.

Obviously death by hanging or strangulation was out of the question. And drinking something poisonous such as Draino had minimal appeal for her. What she wanted was something quick acting and relatively pain free.

Suddenly, Babe eyed the knife in her hand. All she had to do was slam it once into her heart and that would be that. But try as hard as she might, she couldn't bring herself to strike a blow. And so she flung the knife away from her in frustration and turned toward the stove. Hadn't she been warned all her life to make sure to light the old gas oven on account of a person could die from inhaling the fumes if it weren't lit?

Pleased by the thought of death by inhalation of fumes far more than by thoughts of death by stabbing, Babe hurried toward the stove and turned the oven on. She stared at the oven door anxiously, wondering how long it would take for the fumes to get sufficiently noxious. "Come on," she told the oven. "Come on. Hurry up! I beg of you . . . *Hurry up!*"

Babe counted silently to ten and then flung the oven door open. She gulped hard and started to put her head inside, but the oven rack blocked her entrance. She hurled the rack across the room with all her might, then thrust her head as far back into the oven as she could and breathed deeply.

It was darker and scarier inside the oven than Babe had expected it to be. She looked around at the various charred bits of food at the sides and tried to concentrate on them rather than on the thought that the darkness she was hating now was going to be with her for eternity.

Moments passed—the longest moments of Babe's life—and yet death didn't seem to be coming. Babe drummed her fingertips on top of the stove. "Oh please," she urged the oven. But still she remained alive and alone in her dark world.

At last Babe couldn't stand waiting any longer and decided to explode herself by lighting the oven with her head still inside the thing. She knew it wasn't a terribly nice way to go, but desperation had seized her and she began to grope blindly about the stove for some matches. Finally finding a box, she reached inside it for a match, but the dizziness she was feeling from the oven fumes was making her clumsy, and no matter how many matches she struck, she couldn't get a single one to light.

Her head was throbbing and she could feel her brain turning cloudy and strange. The gas hissed at her and soon she began to hallucinate that she was seeing a door open far away from her. A woman appeared at the doorframe with a bushy yellow cat at her side. Babe watched dreamily as the woman closed the door behind her and began walking with the cat down a flight of stairs that let her deeper and deeper into a darkness as eerie and frightening as the darkness inside Babe's oven. For the longest time Babe couldn't make out the woman's face, could only see her in shadows, skinny and scared looking, but then the woman reached the bottom of the stairs and turned toward Babe and Babe saw that the woman was her mother.

"Oh please, Mama, please!" Babe called out, wanting her mother to reach for her hand and take her with her. But her mother turned away from her as though she couldn't hear Babe's cry and began to feel her way through the pitch-black cellar of her Vicksburg home, past the washing machine, the canned fruit jars, the boxes of winter clothes and Christmas ornaments, until she finally came to a clothesline.

Groggily Babe watched her mother touch the thick rope and then reach down for the yellow cat. Babe expected her mother to lift up the cat and wrap his neck in the clothesline, but that wasn't what happened at all. Instead her mother gave the cat a pet and a kiss and said, "Shoo boy, scat!" But the cat didn't leave. It stayed at her side as she began to climb onto a stool and place her own neck into a knotted section of the rope. And then, just as the noose began to go tight on her neck, her eyes became huge with terror and she looked with fearful desperation at the cat. . . .

Suddenly Babe became very excited and she yelled out, "Mama! Mama! So that's why you done it!" And, drugged and delirious, she tried to stand up. Immediately her head crashed against the ceiling of the oven and she keeled over, unconscious, her head still in the darkness of the oven.

For a moment, the entire house seemed to come to a halt, as though it, too, had been knocked lifeless. Gas hissed through the kitchen, spilled through each room of what had once been a sunny, cheerful home. But then, just as the last moments of day flickered through the windows, the back door of the house opened and Meg walked into the kitchen carrying a huge bakery box.

Meg sniffed once at the air, then glanced toward the stove. She screamed the moment she saw her sister sprawled across the oven and raced to her.

"Babe!" Meg cried out, dumping her box down and quickly pulling Babe's head from the oven. "Oh my God! What are you doing? What the hell are you doing?"

Babe gazed dizzily up at her sister. "Nothing," she whispered. "I don't know. Nothing."

Meg turned the gas off and moved Babe toward a chair. "Sit down." But Babe didn't seem to hear her. "Will you sit *down*!"

Limply Babe slid into the chair. "I'm okay," she murmured.

"Put your head between your knees and breathe deep," Meg ordered.

But Babe had something she needed to say and didn't obey her sister. "Meg . . ."

"Just do it!" Meg shouted. "I'll get you some water."

Reluctantly Babe tucked her head between her legs while Meg ran to the sink for a glass of water. But the moment Meg brought her the glass, Babe sat up again and stared at her sister with astonishment shining in her eyes. "Meg . . ." she said again.

Meg dropped into the chair next to Babe's. "Yes?"

"I know why she did it," Babe whispered excitedly.

Meg wiped at her own forehead. "What? Why who did what?"

Babe smiled joyfully. "*Mama.* I know why she hung that cat along with her."

Meg's eyes went wide. "You *do*?"

Babe nodded. "It's 'cause she was afraid of dying all alone."

"Was she?"

Leaning close to her sister, Babe nodded again. "She felt so unsure, you know, as to what was coming. It seemed the best thing coming up would be a lot of angels and all of them singing. But I imagine they have high, scary voices and little gold pointed fingers that are as sharp as blades and you don't want to meet 'em all alone. So it wasn't like what people was saying about her hating that cat. She *needed* him with her 'cause she felt so all alone."

Meg looked at Babe for a long time, then stared at the oven. "Oh Babe," she finally whispered. "Why, Babe? *Why?*"

"Why what?"

"Why did you stick your head in the oven?"

Babe sighed and shrugged. "I don't know, Meg. I'm having a bad day. It's been a *real* bad day. Those pictures and Willie Jay heading north and . . ." Suddenly Babe's whole body began to tremble, and her voice turned shaky: "Zackery called me up. He says he's gonna have me classified insane and then send me on out to Whitfield Asylum."

"What!" Meg said indignantly. "Why, he could *never* do that!"

"Why not?"

" 'Cause you're not insane."

Babe frowned. "I'm not?"

"No! He's trying to bluff you. Ha! Him calling *you* insane." And here, Meg leaned back in her chair and said with utter confidence, "Why, you're just as perfectly sane as anyone walking the streets of Hazlehurst, Mississippi."

But Babe wasn't too sure about this. "I am?" she asked nervously.

Meg reached over to her little sister. "More so! A *lot* more so!"

Babe smiled with relief. She had great respect for Meg's opinion on matters, and if Meg thought her sane, by God then she must be sane. "Good!" she said happily.

And yet things weren't quite so settled for Meg. Looking Babe clearly in the eyes, she said, "But Babe. We've just got to learn how to get through these bad days. I mean it's getting to be a *thing* in our family." And then, more quietly, she went on, "And you're not like Mama. You're not all alone."

Babe looked at her sister and smiled. "I'm not," she agreed.

The sisters grinned at each other a moment, then reached for each other and embraced for some time. "No, you're not," Meg whispered. And then, pulling back, she looked around the kitchen. "Where's Lenny?"

Babe shrugged as Meg glanced out the window. She could see Lenny walking toward the house carrying a basket full of pawpaws. "Wait!" Meg shouted excitedly. "There she is." And Meg raced toward the door and ran out to the back steps.

Lenny was walking freer and stronger than Meg had ever seen her walk before in her life. So confident did her sister appear that at first Meg found it hard to believe it *was* Lenny. But then Lenny looked at her and Meg began waving back. "Lenny! Oh Lenny!"

Lenny glanced at Meg curiously.

"Come on!" Meg shouted. "Hurry up! There's something in the kitchen!"

"What?" Lenny asked.

Meg glanced behind her. She could see Babe in the kitchen hurriedly opening the bakery box Meg had brought with her. "I don't know!" Meg shouted at Lenny. "Come see."

Babe came running out the back door. "It's big!" she yelled. "Hurry up!"

Lenny looked at her sisters with puzzlement as they ran toward her eagerly, grabbed her hands, and began hurrying her along to the house. All three of the sisters laughed as they banged open the door to the screened-in porch and pushed on toward the kitchen.

Suddenly Meg shoved her hands over Lenny's eyes. "What!" Lenny cried out. "What is it? What?!"

Meg led Lenny right up to the bakery box and then dropped her hands. The first thing Lenny saw as she opened her eyes was a gigantic, beautifully decorated cake with white icing, red trim, and thirty burning candles.

"Surprise!" Meg and Babe yelled. "Happy birthday to Lenny!"

Lenny's eyes filled with tears as she read the message on her cake. HAPPY BIRTHDAY TO LENNY—TWO DAYS LATE! "Oh, no!" she whispered. "Oh, me! What a surprise! I could just cry!"

Babe and Meg looked at their sister with proud joy as Lenny bent over the cake excitedly. "Oh look," she said, and pointed happily at each word on her cake as she read the message out loud. "How cute!" And then, as she took in the candles Babe had set burning for her, "My! Will you *look* at all those candles . . . it's absolutely *frightening*!"

"Oh, no, Lenny," Babe said, "it's *good*! 'Cause . . ."—and here Babe had to wait for a moment for divine inspiration to strike her as to just why so many candles were good—" 'cause the more candles you have on your cake, the stronger your wish is."

"Really?" Lenny asked.

Babe smiled with absolute faith in her own logic. "Sure!"

Lenny shook her head and stared again at her candles. "Mercy!"

The candles danced brightly on top the whirls of frosting, as Meg and Babe began to sing:

Happy birthday to you
Happy birthday to you
Happy Birthday, dear Lenny
Happy—

Suddenly Lenny waved her hands and interrupted the song. "Oh, but wait!" she cried out. "I . . . I can't think of my wish! My body's gone all nervous inside."

Meg turned to her sister impatiently. "Oh for God's sake, Lenny. Come *on*!"

But Lenny couldn't "come on." She kept staring at her cake, amazed by all the shining lights, and especially amazed that her sisters had thought to celebrate her birthday with such a spectacular cake. Never had she been the recipient of so much attention, so much affection. Only two days before, she had been alone in the world, making her desperate wishes on a crumbled cookie, and now here she was with Babe and Meg at her side, Charlie on his way to Hazlehurst, and a gleaming birthday cake just before her eyes.

"The wax is all melting," Babe urged.

Lenny brought her hands to her head in frustration. "My mind is just a blank, a total blank!"

Meg couldn't believe her sister was taking the whole thought of a birthday wish so seriously. "Will you please just *do* it!"

Babe hopped up and down, thrilled to be

somewhere other than the oven, eager to watch her big sister blow the candles out. "Lenny, hurry! Come on!"

"Okay! Okay!" Lenny shouted, still not knowing what her wish would be. "Just go!"

Once more Meg and Babe began to sing the Happy Birthday song. Babe sang loudly, her heart in the right place even though some of her notes weren't, while Meg's voice soared with harmony and beauty. Lenny looked at her sisters for a moment and thought of how much the three of them had been through together—Daddy's desertion, Mama's horrible decline and death, Old Grandmama's harsh ways, the stares of the townspeople, Old Grandaddy's coma, Babe's arrest, Meg's loss of her singing voice, Lenny's own troubles with men . . . so much bleak sadness the three of them had endured, and yet here they were, still together and hoping for the future.

Lenny closed her eyes, but still she could see her sisters' faces. Babe . . . For so long Lenny had considered her youngest sister a child, had pictured Babe as a kind of happy-go-lucky creature from a fairy tale, made to be petted and fussed over, but all that time Babe had been growing up. Babe had kept struggling, kept smiling in spite of her terrible marriage, and now she was getting free from that marriage, blossoming. Babe, Lenny knew, would someday blow a beautiful note from her used saxophone—a note that would be as clear and strong and full of love as Babe herself. And Meg . . . For so many years Lenny had thought Meg hated her. All the fights the two sisters had had. All the jealousy Lenny had felt about Meg's singing, about Meg's ways with men. What had all that been about? Now Lenny could feel Meg at her side, could almost touch the love Meg was sending her way. Meg hadn't hated Lenny at all. She'd just been struggling like Lenny herself, trying to find a place in the world. Lenny listened to her sister's angelic voice and knew that voice was going to keep on singing, wasn't ever going to lose its way again.

Lenny breathed as deep as she could and felt down into the very center of her heart for a wish. Finally, her face glimmering in the light of the candles, she leaned forward and blew out all thirty of her lights.

Meg and Babe burst into applause as Lenny opened her eyes again and grinned at her cake, triumphant to see that she had been able to blow out all her candles with one breath. So maybe—if she'd made her wish strong enough—it had had a chance of coming true.

"Oh you made it!" Meg told her, giving her arm a squeeze.

"Hurray!" Babe shouted.

Lenny laughed. "Oh me! Oh me! I hope that wish comes true. I hope it does."

"Why?" Babe asked. "What did you wish for?"

Lenny bent down over her cake and carefully began to remove her candles, trying as hard as she could not to disturb all the pretty frosting. "Why, I can't tell you that," she said to Babe.

Babe grinned. "Oh sure you can."

But Lenny stood her ground. "Oh no! Then it won't come true."

Ever the expert on birthday wishes, Babe strenuously disagreed. "Why that's just superstition," she told Lenny. "Of course it will, if you made it deep enough." And leaning over to her sister and imploring her with all her charm, "Now come on and tell us. What was it you wished for?"

"Yes, tell us," Meg said. "What was it?"

Lenny looked at her sisters hesitantly. She didn't even know how to begin to put her wish into words. It wasn't like the wishes she had made the other morning. Not for a particular *thing* to come true. She frowned a bit and tried to explain to her sisters. "Well, I guess, it wasn't really a specific wish. This . . . this vision just sort of came into my mind."

"A vision?" Babe asked, thinking back on her own vision of Mama and wondering if Lenny had seen the same thing. "What was it of?"

Staring around the kitchen, Lenny's eyes became dreamy. "I don't know exactly," she whispered as she looked from the window where the old rope swing was still swaying to the rickety white table where her cake was waiting to be eaten. "It was something about the three of us smiling and laughing together, but it wasn't for every minute. Just this one moment and we were all laughing."

Babe looked puzzled. "What were we laughing about?"

Lenny shrugged. "I don't know. Just nothing, I guess."

Babe continued to look a bit uncertain about whether Lenny's vision qualified as a genuine birthday wish, but Meg understood and turned to Lenny with a smile. "Well," she said quietly, "that's a nice wish to make."

For a few moments Meg and Lenny stared at each other. Their eyes—for the first time—were able to see past each other's differences and to the places in their hearts where their love and faith in each other burned strong and eternal. And then Meg grinned and said, "Here, now, I'll get a knife so we can go ahead and cut the cake in celebration of Lenny being born."

Lenny grinned back at Meg as her sister ran to the silverware drawer. She liked the way Meg had described the occasion: a celebration of her *birth*. No more would she let herself live like a frightened ostrich with her head in the ground. From this day forward she was going to stand tall and grab for the stars in the sky. And if people didn't like the new Lenny, if they tried to make her feel timid and clumsy and mousy, why she would just take her broom and sweep them off into the heavens where they couldn't bother her anymore!

Babe watched as Meg ran back to the table and handed a knife to Lenny. It seemed odd that just a few minutes ago she'd been thinking of stabbing herself to death with such a knife. Life could be very strange sometimes—one second you're wanting to drop dead, the next second you're wanting to eat birthday cake. It made no sense in a way, but at least it kept things exciting . . . if you managed to keep from killing yourself during the bad times.

"Give each one of us a rose," Babe instructed Lenny. "A whole rose apiece."

Lenny began to slice the cake. "Well, I'll try . . . I'll *try.*"

Meg licked at the icing. Tomorrow she would be back on the bus, returning to Hollywood. She sighed at the thought of having to face her job at the dog food company. But that would just be temporary. Now that she had found her voice in Hazlehurst she could audition for singing jobs. And who knew? Maybe someday she really would have that house with a heart-shaped swimming pool. Maybe Babe and Lenny could all come out to visit her someday and she could introduce them to all the movie stars—who by that time would be her friends. Why not? Miracles did have a way of happening sometimes . . . "Mmmm," she told her sisters. "This icing is delicious." And offering a fingerful to Babe: "Here. Try some."

Babe lapped at the icing and giggled. "Mmmmmm! It's wonderful." And then she, too, scooped her fingers into the cake. "Here, Lenny."

Lenny laughed joyously as she licked at Babe's fingers. This was turning out to be the best birthday party of her life. The cake was perfect; her sisters were happy; and best of all, the three of them were together, right now, in this kitchen. She sliced off three enormous slabs from the cake and tossed them to Babe and Meg. Her sisters caught their pieces in the air and burst into greedy giggles as they ravenously attacked the cake.

Lenny's eyes were shining with joy. "Oh, how I do love birthday cake," she whispered. "How I *do.*"

A breeze blew through the kitchen window,

and with it seemed to come the sounds of a saxophone playing a song full of the Magrath sisters' future—a bold, triumphant tune. All three women stood for a moment laughing and eating cake, their faces golden, shimmering with the magical glow of a wish come true.